Learning About Sex

Jennifer J. Aho
& John W. Petras

LEARNING ABOUT SEX

A Guide for Children and Their Parents

illustrated by Jennifer J. Aho

Holt, Rinehart and Winston · New York

Printed in the United States of America

10 9 8 7 6 5 4

Library of Congress Cataloging in Publication Data

Aho, Jennifer J.
    Learning about sex.

    Includes index.
    1. Sex instruction. 2. Sexual ethics.
I. Petras, John W., joint author. II. Title.
HQ57.A35   613.9′5   78-53949
ISBN 0-03-043966-3 Paperback
ISBN 0-03-045666-5 Hardbound

ISBN 0-03-043966-3

for Trevor Michael

Contents

For Parents

Our experience in conducting sex education workshops and sexuality classes has shown that children and young people prefer parents as a source of sex education. Regrettably, however, parents often do not play a significant role. Since that is the case, we hope this book can provide you with a framework for relating factual information to your child within the context of your own individual value system.

If children are to feel comfortable with sexuality, they must first feel comfortable about their body. A child should be taught that although there is a difference between boys and girls, a penis or a vagina is not better or worse, or more or less than the other. It is especially important for your child to learn that his or her sexual organs are not "dirty" or "unclean." A child's questions about his or her body, whether sexual or nonsexual, should always be answered in a direct way.

The changing body is another area of concern. Adults easily forget that changes in the body around age twelve can be a source of worry and embarrassment. To eliminate needless concern, prepare your child for these changes before they occur.

Your role in explaining the processes of puberty is to help your child look forward to the changes that signal the onset of adulthood. In your discussions with your child, you may find it helpful to share some of your own experiences of growing up.

Point out that although bodily changes are characteristic of all people, they do not necessarily occur at the same time for everyone. Girls begin to menstruate at different times, some earlier, some later. Some boys will experience ejaculation before others of their age. Your child needs the assurance that such a time difference is normal and something to be expected. You may, for example, wish to compare these changes to such other natural processes as acquiring gray hair or learning to walk.

Preparing girls for breast development, the appearance of hair under the arms and around the vagina, and their first menstruation can save needless embarrassment and worry. They should be informed that the menstrual cycle may vary somewhat, and that this is nothing to be concerned about. The point to be made about menstruation is that it is a normal and natural process, that it earmarks the beginning of womanhood, and that pregnancy is now possible.

As a boy enters puberty, his voice may crack, whiskers may begin to grow, hair appears under the arms and around the penis, and testicles begin to produce sperm. Boys need to be assured that the ejaculation of semen during periods of sleep or sexual excitement is a normal occurrence. The point to emphasize is that the body's production of sperm is the indicator that physiologically the boy is now a man.

The growing process provides excellent examples of how the human body changes continually throughout life. Menopause is another such example. Children can learn that bodies change and these changes affect the reproductive part of sex, but not the pleasure aspects of it. The naturalness of sex can be seen in the fact that sexual pleasure is possible for a lifetime, while reproduction is limited to only a part of it. There is no reason for your child to grow up believing in the myth of the sexless older years.

Masturbation

Masturbation is one of the earliest and most effective ways in which your child can learn about his or her body. Masturbation provides the earliest expression of curiosity about one's physical self and is the first learning experience of the pleasures and joys of sexuality. It is a normal part of the celebration of the human body. Your reaction to masturbation can influence your child's sexual development. That is why it is important for you to accept the naturalness and normality of masturbation.

In the past (perhaps when you were a child), attitudes about masturbation stressed guilt and certain alleged harmful effects. People had the mistaken belief that it was abnormal. We now know that there is a positive relationship between masturbation and sexual fulfillment in our later years. Women who were taught that masturbation was

10

something "nice girls didn't do" often have uncomfortable feelings about their body, keeping them from attaining their natural right to sexual fulfillment as adults.

Male masturbation has always been more acceptable. Even so, the guilt and secrecy surrounding it made for rapid ejaculation. This can become dysfunctional in later life, as is evident by the number of men who suffer from premature ejaculation, preventing them and their partners from achieving sexual happiness.

Many parents fear that if they present a positive image of masturbation to their child, the child will want to do it all the time, sometimes at embarrassing and inappropriate moments. If you allow children privacy this will not be a problem. Further, children allowed privacy at home also develop a respect for the privacy of others.

Feelings

Since most of us were raised with the idea that sex was not a nice subject to learn or talk about, many people are embarrassed by their sexual feelings. **All** feelings for others develop in the context of a relationship. Sexual feelings are no different. We recognize our feelings when we are angry with someone, or pleased, or happy. But we often pretend that sexual feelings do not exist. They are only one of the many different types of feelings we have for one another.

Feelings and relationships are often difficult to discuss. Even people who are close to one another may find it hard to talk about the feelings they have for each other. The fact that we have different feelings for different people is something children need to understand. Otherwise they are forced to make sense out of the many conflicting messages they receive. When you consider the portrayal of relationships on television, it is easy to see how confusing this can be.

Your relationship with your child is the logical starting point for any discussion of feelings and relationships. Parents and children develop a certain relationship. Use the feelings you and your child have for each other as an example. You might ask your child to think about the different relationships he or she has with best friends, casual friends, classmates, and nonfriends. Then talk about the differences between the feelings for each of these people and how the relationships and feelings go together. The relationship between you and your spouse, or some other significant person, can be used as an example in opening a discussion about feelings.

It is also important to let your child know that bad feelings are as natural as good ones. We all become angry at times, often with people we love. Talk about how parents become angrier with their own children than with other children because of the love they feel for them. Let your child know that he or she can discuss all feelings, good **or** bad, with you. Discussing unpleasant feelings openly is preferable to burying them and leaving them to erupt at some future time.

Your child should be given to understand that in some relationships between adults, sex becomes a way of expressing the feelings of love the adults have for one another. Husbands and wives engage in sexual intercourse. For many adults in a close relationship sex becomes a way of expressing a commitment. Try to give your child the impression that both men and women enjoy intercourse and that neither is necessarily active or passive. Stress that intercourse is a cooperative activity of both the woman and the man. Sex is only one part of a single relationship. It is not characteristic of most of our relationships. Usually, it is not the most important dimension of any relationship.

Children learn about many activities long before it is considered appropriate for them to do so. Children reading this book may not yet be sexually mature, and may not have had to deal with strong sexual feelings. Let your child know that whenever questions do arise, he or she can bring up the subject again.

Let your child know what values you expect him or her to use in guiding future behavior. A parent and child discussion on feelings and relationships is one of the best ways to strengthen your role as the major source of guidance for your child.

Sexual Intercourse

Books, parents, or peers may leave the child with the belief that sexual activity invariably leads to pregnancy. But children learn that not everyone who engages in sexual intercourse becomes pregnant. If parents tell them otherwise, children feel they are being given slanted information. The result will be to call into question the parent's credibility in other areas as well. Studies indicate that attempting to scare children with the threat of pregnancy serves only to keep teens from using birth control methods but does not prevent them from acting out what they see as "natural" sexual behavior.

Children find it natural to want to discuss the act of intercourse and may wonder why people find it such a difficult subject to talk about. Be honest. In today's world children are aware of the fact that people have intercourse for reasons other than making babies. It is up to you to articulate the values that will aid in guiding your child's future sexual activity.

Reproduction

In this book, your child will read about the physical differences and similarities between males and females, the nature of sexual intercourse, sperm production and menstruation, and the tie between relationships and feelings. By making reproduction a part of human sexuality, we believe the information will be more meaningful and worthwhile for you and your child. Reproduction, body development, feelings, and sexual intercourse are all treated separately. This will enable you to elaborate on the relevance of the physical aspects of reproduction, as well as discuss the parenting dimension of childbirth. Children find reproduction fascinating. Unfortunately, the subject is greatly misunderstood by them.

As adults, our bodies offer us direct evidence of human sexuality. For a woman, menstruation is a real part of life, as are concerns about pregnancy. For a man, sperm production and concern over parenthood are real. Since the immature bodies of children do not provide this explicit evidence, your patience and understanding are called for.

In discussing reproduction with your child, we suggest a technique that has proven effective with other children. Allow your child ample time to ask a question. Before answering, ask your child to tell you what he or she believes the correct answer to be. You will then receive an indication of what your child already knows, as well as the types of misinformation to which he or she has been exposed. More important, this approach makes you and your child active partners in exploring the material together. By listening to your child explain what he or she thinks is correct and then discussing the answer, you are more likely to be respected as a credible source of sexual information. Take nothing for granted in your discussions. What seems clear to you now was once a source of confusion.

In the past, learning about reproduction was viewed as the most important part of sex education. It was common to leave the explanation of intercourse at the level of "planting a seed" by the father. Today, children learn about sex in many different ways, and not only with respect to reproduction. It seems to us that you will want your child to learn about this significant activity from the point of view of **your** values, not those of peers or the mass media.

Formerly, human sexuality was viewed as an unfit subject for children. Reproduction among plants and animals was presented as a preliminary to explaining human behavior. We now know that this approach does little more than confuse a child, as well as inadvertently devalue the uniqueness of human sexuality. To teach your child that human sex is patterned after plant and animal sex is to imply that personal responsibility is not important. Plants and animals do not consider the consequences of their actions.

You will find that each child has his or her own specific questions to discuss. However, a discussion of pregnancy will be of interest to almost any child.

A common interest for most children is knowing how the baby is able to grow inside the mother's body. While you may be tempted to say "the stomach," this can cause needless worry and misinformation. The child knows that everything that enters the stomach either stays in the body or leaves by elimination. Simply tell the child the baby grows in the uterus—an organ inside the mother's body that grows with the baby.

It is important for a child to recognize that for humans, unlike animals, a lengthy period of care is needed after birth. Discuss parenting before and after birth. The importance of the father in the life of the infant has been recognized only recently. Point out to your child how his or her parenting, whatever it may be (perhaps you are a single parent), offers him or her the love, attention, and guidance that are necessary for all children.

Birth Control

We know from studies that the presence or absence of a sex education has little effect upon the child's level of sexual activity. Whether or not a child engages in sexual behavior is unrelated to what he or she is learning about sex or whether it is being taught in school. Being a natural function of life, sex is discovered by most children early in their lives. Unless precautions are taught regarding the misuse of sex, all other education is meaningless.

Despite this, a myth which is still popular among some people says that if you teach children about birth control, they will view this as a free rein to have sex. Evidence shows that this is not true. Children who receive birth control information are more likely to be responsible for their sexuality. Since the number of pregnancies among unmarried teen-agers is greater than ever before (300 percent higher than at the turn of the century) it is essential that your child be informed of ways in which unwanted pregnancies can be prevented. The earlier this information is taught, the more certain that knowledge is to influence his or her attitude about sexuality when sexual expression is appropriate.

Venereal Disease

One out of every five seniors graduating from high school this year will contact some form of venereal disease. Gonorrhea is the number one reported communicable disease in the country. The most rapid rise in VD rates is among eleven- to fourteen-year-olds. Clearly, VD is a serious health problem for the young. Despite advances in treatment, VD has continued to rise for a number of reasons. The condom or rubber has been replaced by the pill as the leading form of birth control. Unlike the condom, the pill offers no protection against VD. The rise can also be attributed to the lack of comprehensive sex education programs, parental negligence in educating children, and the circulation of myths.

The myths about VD are well-known: It is shameful, dirty, or even a form of punishment for engaging in sexual activity. Such myths lead to the belief that ordinary people don't get VD. More important, the idea that VD is shameful has prevented many people from seeking treatment. As in all matters of sexuality, falsehoods and shame do not prevent people from engaging in sexual activity. Instead, because they feel guilty, people may refrain from taking such necessary actions as seeing a physician or using a condom, which remind them that they are sexual beings.

If left untreated, certain types of VD can cause serious harm. There is also the danger of birth defects in children born of infected pregnant women. The need for education in this area is essential, since many of the people who contact VD do not exhibit any clearly recognizable symptoms and may inadvertently pass it on to others through sexual contact.

Let your child know that VD is a disease that can be prevented and cured. Just as children are aware that they may become ill by coming into contact with ill people, so too can they understand that an illness associated with sexual intercourse can be contacted through inter-course. It is not necessary for you to go into a great deal of detail with your child regarding the various forms of VD.

Children have contact daily with information about VD and the availability of treatment. There are popular songs about VD, as well as sayings and expressions, most of which have grown out of efforts by health departments to control the spread of the disease. If your child is older, say of high school age, he or she has access to free publications through local health departments or your state department of health. Anyone may call this toll-free telephone number for information: 800-523-1885.

Sex Offenders

Any realistic parent and child discussion on sexuality requires that the subject of sex offenders be mentioned. With recent publicity and educational programs, you need not assume that you are discussing a subject that is completely alien to your child. Also, you need not focus upon **sex** offenders. Children should be taught never to go anywhere with strangers and to report any attempts made to entice them into autos.

Reactions of horror and shame by parents can do more harm to children than an encounter with a sex offender. Be realistic. Don't attempt to scare your child into believing that sex offenders are dirty, mean, and old. These stereotypes are false. They are also misleading.

Sex offenders are not easily identified. Those few adults who perceive children in a sexual way come from all walks of life. Most child molesters are heterosexual (prefers the opposite sex). Only a few are homosexual (prefers the same sex). In fact, most sex offenders are not strangers, but are family friends, neighbors, or relatives.

We recognize that you do not wish to cause your child undue concern. A discussion of sex offenders ought to be carried out in a sensitive and patient fashion. Your child must never be placed in a position of being ashamed to report any type of assault. By attempting to frighten your child, you may instill in him or her a sense of guilt and shame which can have the effect of inhibiting the reporting of an incident. Make it clear that it is not sexual activity that is wrong, but the way it is misused by someone who forces it on another person.

While the actual likelihood of your child's encountering a sex offender is small, a basic education is in order. Ignorance and parental overreaction are the most common dangers threatening children who encounter sex offenders.

Conclusion

During the past few years, there has been a growing movement to re-establish the family as the center of education and child care. Parents are becoming more and more dissatisfied with the results of turning their children over to experts who may not share the parents' value system. Most books aim at replacing the parent's role as the primary source of education for the child. Many currently available books treat the parent as an outsider and present the parent's role as irrelevant. We agree that while a complete presentation is necessary, it cannot be at the expense of the parent's participation in the learning process. A complete sex education involves both facts and values. Parents need to discuss these with their children, and children need to be encouraged to go to their parents. This book is aimed at helping to meet both of these needs.

For Children

This is your book about sex. It is fun to read either alone, or with your parents or some older person whom you feel comfortable with and respect. There are parts in this book for them as well.

Your friends may not have a book like this one and may not know the things you learn here. What they have learned may not be correct. If you have questions, you should ask your parents what they think.

Sex is a fun part of being a person and a natural, normal part of growing up. And that's what this book is all about!

Bodies

People come in all shapes, sizes, and colors. Some are skinny, some are fat, some tall, some short. Some are in wheelchairs, some wear braces, and some people (especially older ones) use walkers and canes. Some bodies are hairy, some smooth; some are old, some young, and some are in between. But everybody is beautiful in his or her own way.

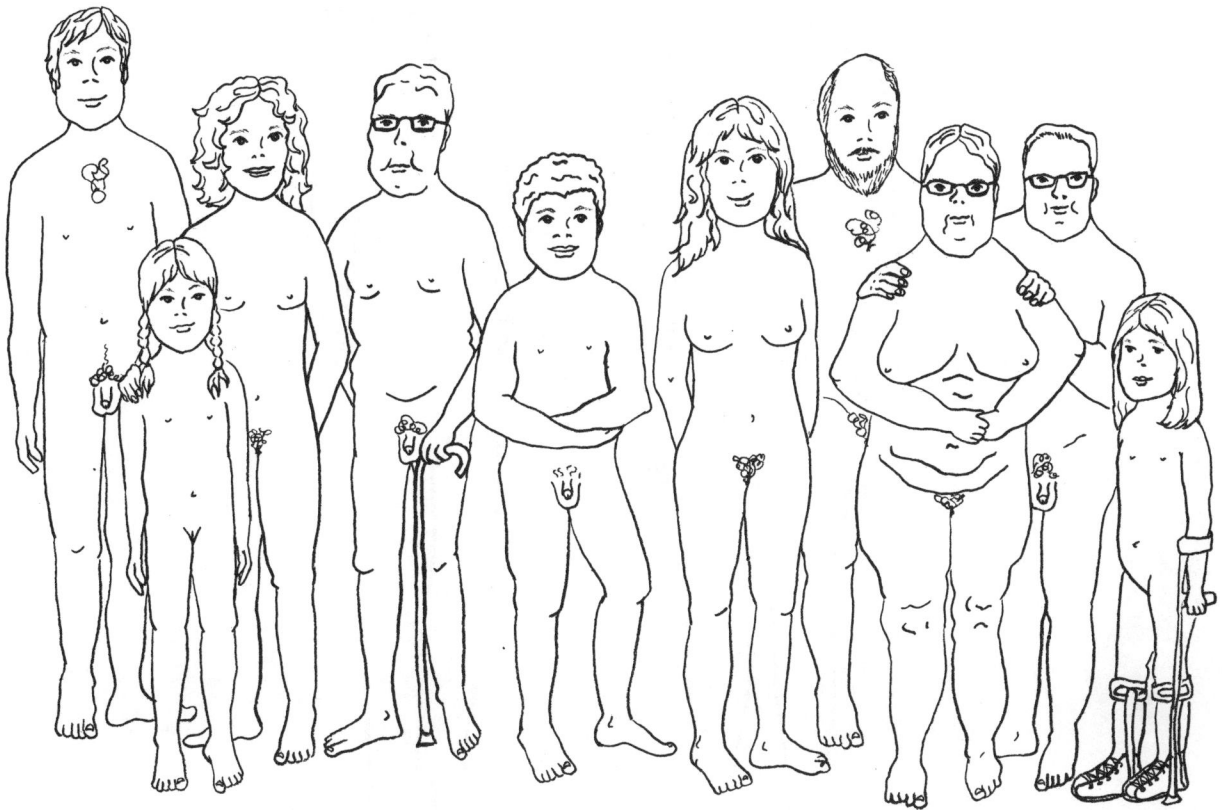

Most of the time, people wear clothes. When they don't you can see the differences between girls and boys and men and women.

Even though bodies are personal and clothes are worn most of the time, all people wonder about their body and whether or not other people's bodies are the same.

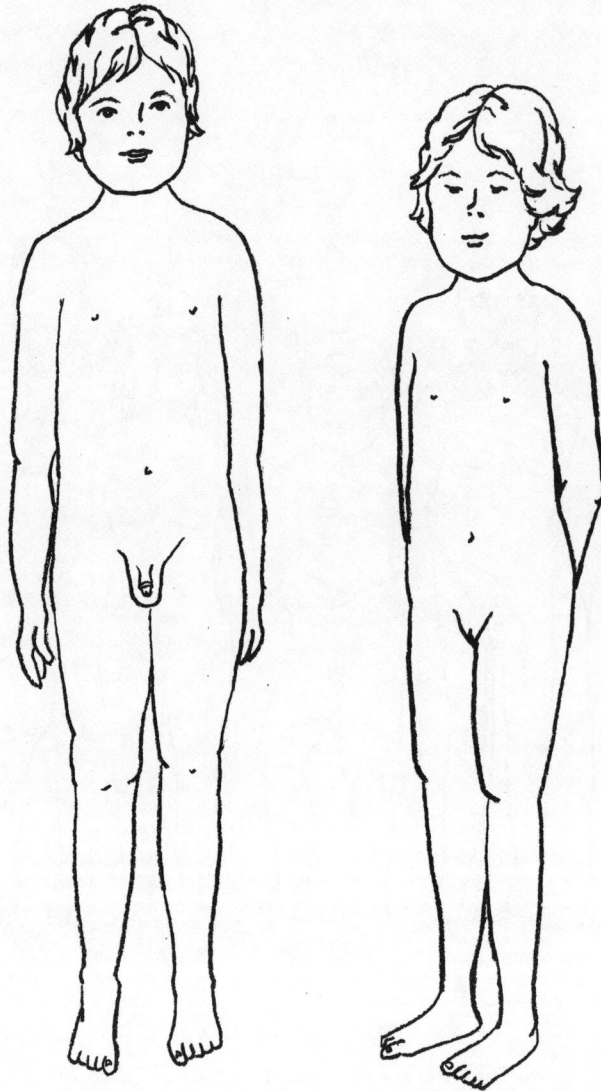

Even if you are not the same color or size or shape as your friends, if you are a boy, you and other boys are the same in an important way. If you are a girl, you may be a different color, size, or shape from other girls, but you are all the same in an important way, and all girls are different from boys.

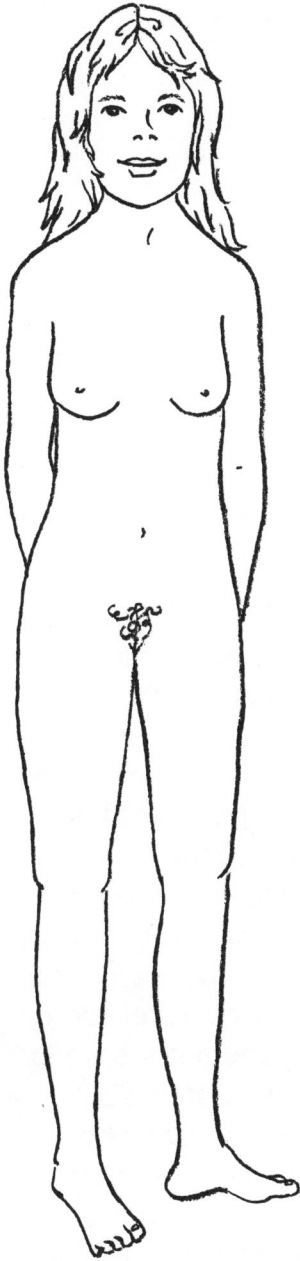
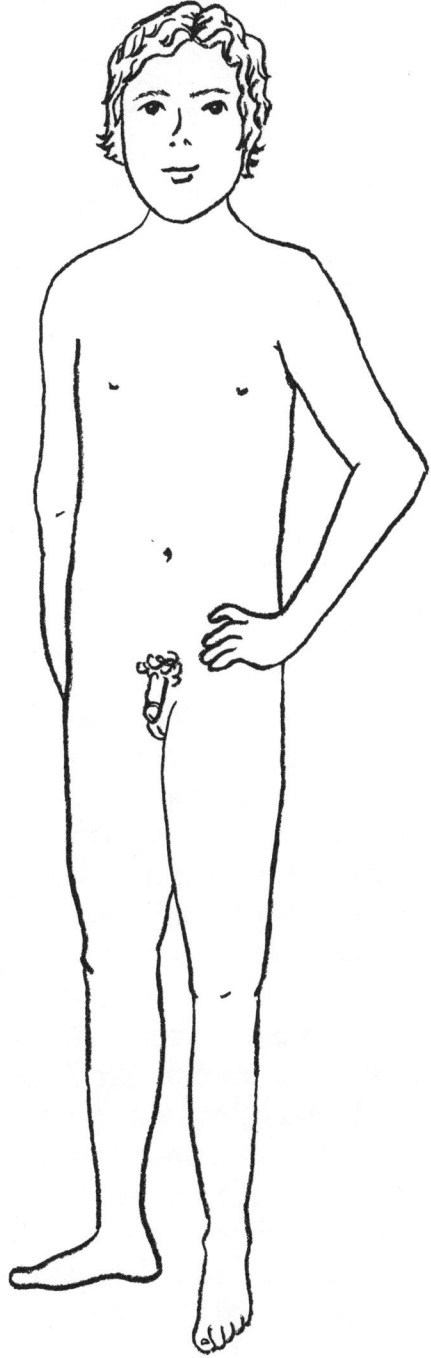

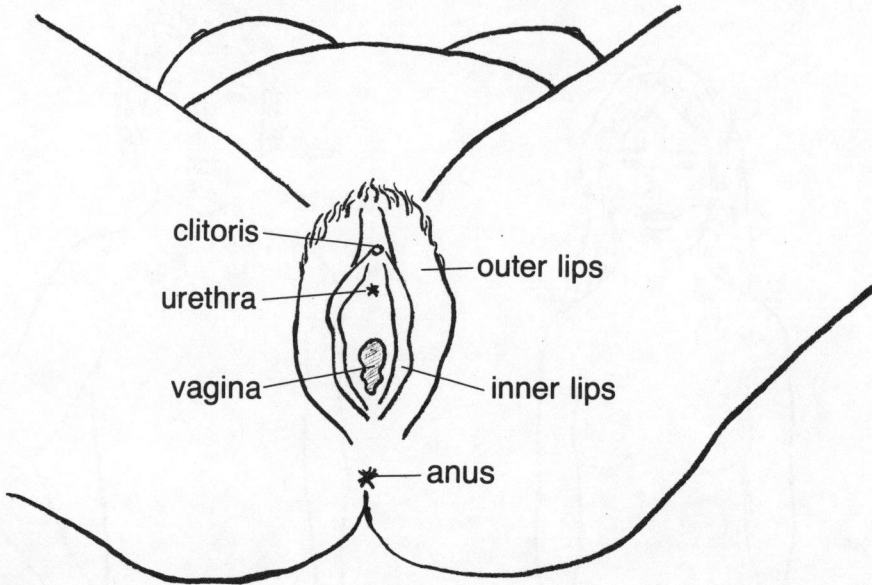

clitoris — outer lips
urethra
vagina — inner lips
anus

Girls

All girls have a *vagina* and a *clitoris*. When a girl gets older, her body grows and her *breasts* begin to get bigger. Hair grows on her body, especially around her vagina and under her arms.

Inside the outer lips of a woman's vagina are two inner lips, a clitoris, and *urethra*. The clitoris is for giving a woman pleasure, and the urethra is a small opening where urine comes out.

As she gets older, something special happens to a girl to let her know she is becoming a woman. She begins *menstruation*. This means that once a month for a few days a bloody discharge will drip out of her vagina. This is also called having a period. Some girls have abdominal cramps, but usually menstruation does not hurt. And it happens to all women everywhere in the world. It tells them that they are grown up. To keep this bloody discharge from getting on her clothes, a woman may use a pad called a *sanitary napkin*, which she can stick to her underpants. Some women would rather use a *tampon*, which is a tiny pad that comes in an applicator and fits inside the woman's vagina. You may have seen sanitary napkins or tampons in your bathroom, in the stores when you go shopping, or advertised on TV.

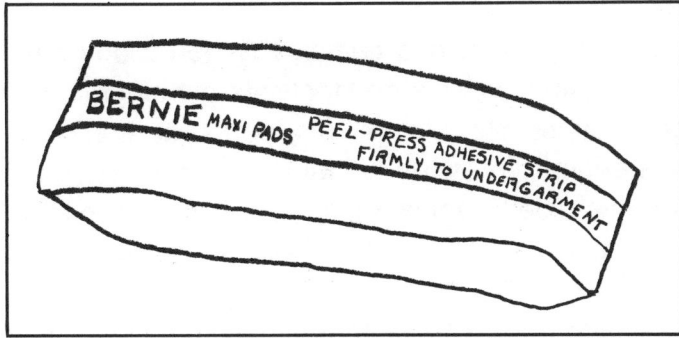

A sanitary napkin

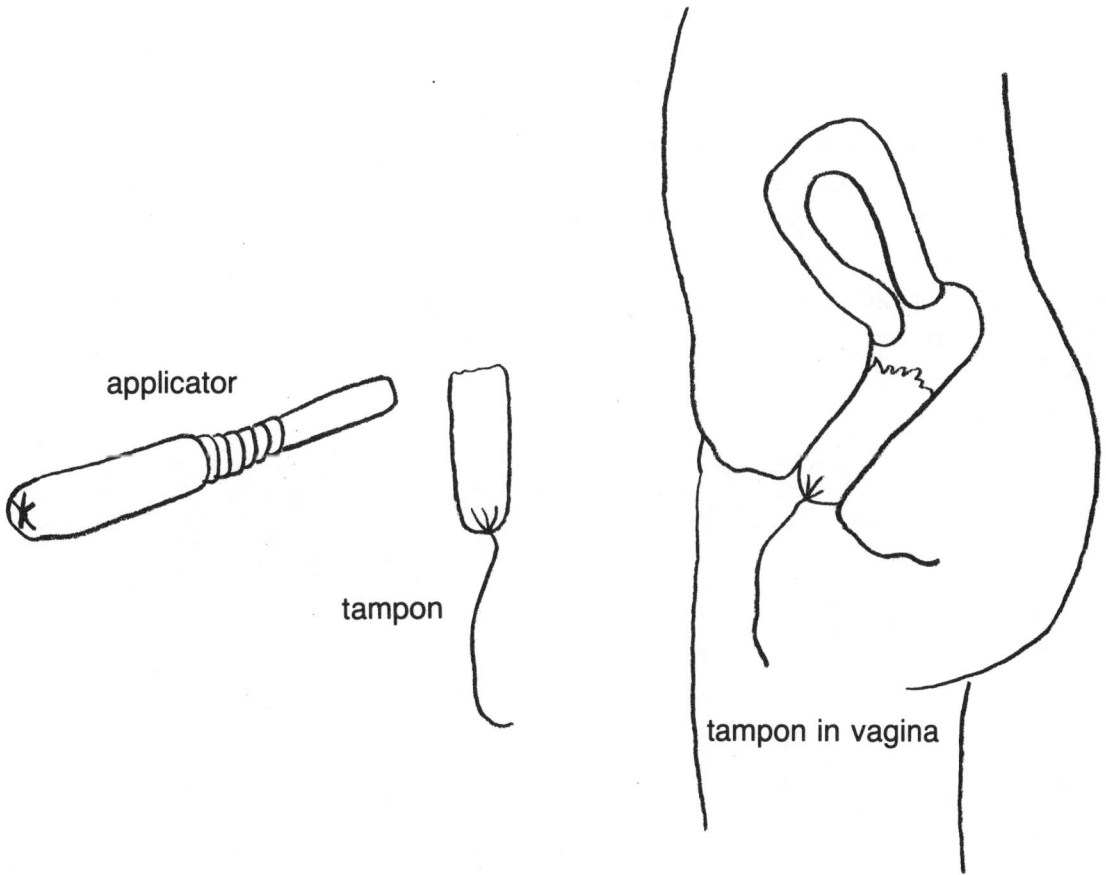

BERNIE MAXI PADS PEEL-PRESS ADHESIVE STRIP FIRMLY TO UNDERGARMENT

applicator

tampon

tampon in vagina

Boys

All boys have a *penis* and *testicles*. When a boy gets older, his body grows and his penis and testicles get bigger. Hair grows on his body, especially around his penis and under his arms. Whiskers begin to grow on his face.

As he gets older, something special happens to let a boy know he is becoming a man. His body begins to produce *semen*, a white sticky stuff that is made inside a boy's body by his *prostate gland*. It mixes with *sperm*, which is made in a boy's testicles, and comes out the end of his penis. The small opening in the end of the penis where urine comes out is the boy's urethra. Semen and sperm come out of the urethra when the penis is stiff. When we say a boy or man has an *erection*, it means that his penis is stiff.

A boy's penis looks the same as every other boy's penis when he is born. But you may have noticed that some penises look different. The reason for this is that some boys have been *circumcised*.

Circumcision means that a few days after a baby boy is born, the doctor removes the *foreskin*, which is the skin that hangs over the end of the penis. Although they may look different, all penises are the same.

Both girls and boys have an *anus*. When we poop, it comes out the anus.

adult circumcised penis   adult uncircumcised penis

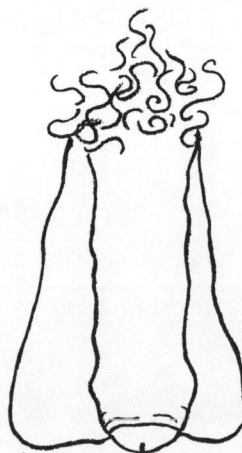

Puberty

Puberty is the word we use when we talk about boys becoming men and girls becoming women. When a boy's body makes semen and sperm and a girl starts to menstruate we say that they have reached puberty. Not all boys and girls reach puberty at the same time. Some boys begin to make semen and sperm in their body several years before other boys. And girls begin to menstruate at different ages too.

What do your mother and father remember about puberty?

As men and women get older, their bodies continue to change.

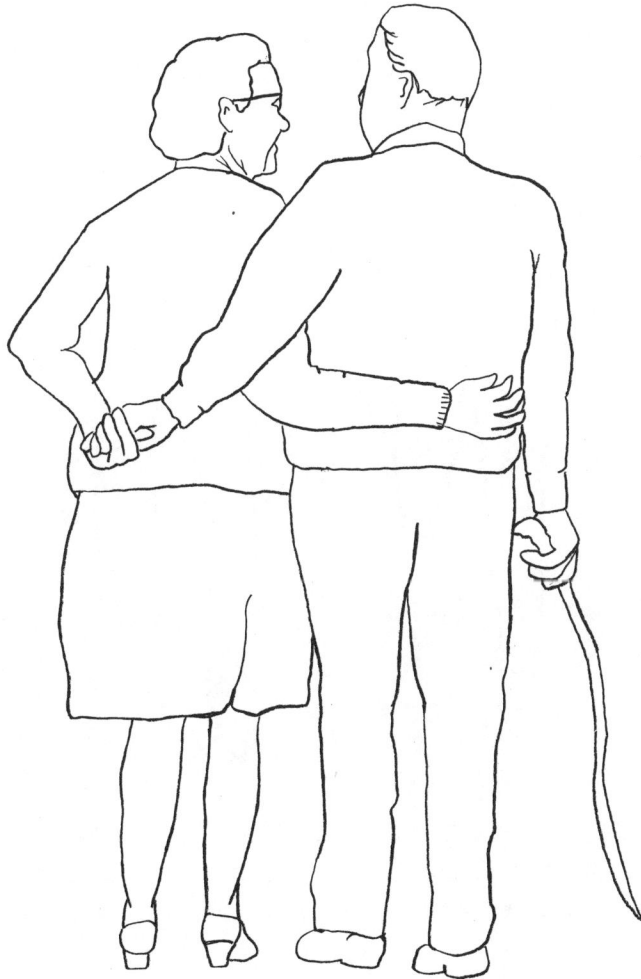

Later in her life, something happens to let a woman know she is still growing. Her menstrual periods stop. The word we use to describe this change is *menopause*. It happens to older women and is a normal and natural part of being a woman.

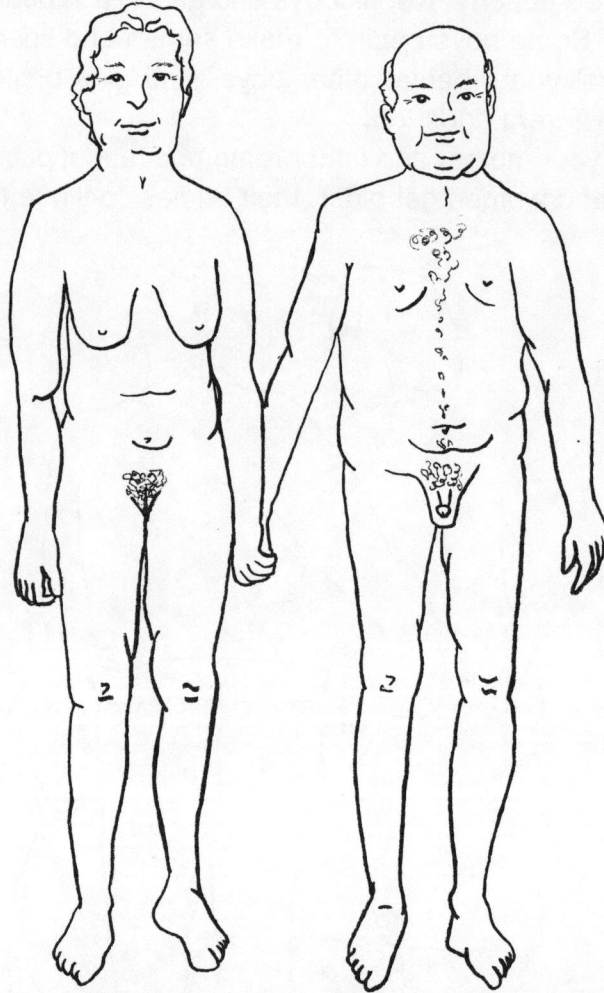

Your body is like a good friend. When your body feels good, you feel good too. You feel good after a good night's sleep, after a bath or shower, when you go to the bathroom, and when you are playing.

On a sunny day, it feels good to lie on the beach or in your yard and feel the warm sun on your body.

It feels good when you hug a soft, friendly dog.

It feels good when you ride a bike or go up high on a swing.

It feels good to have your back rubbed.

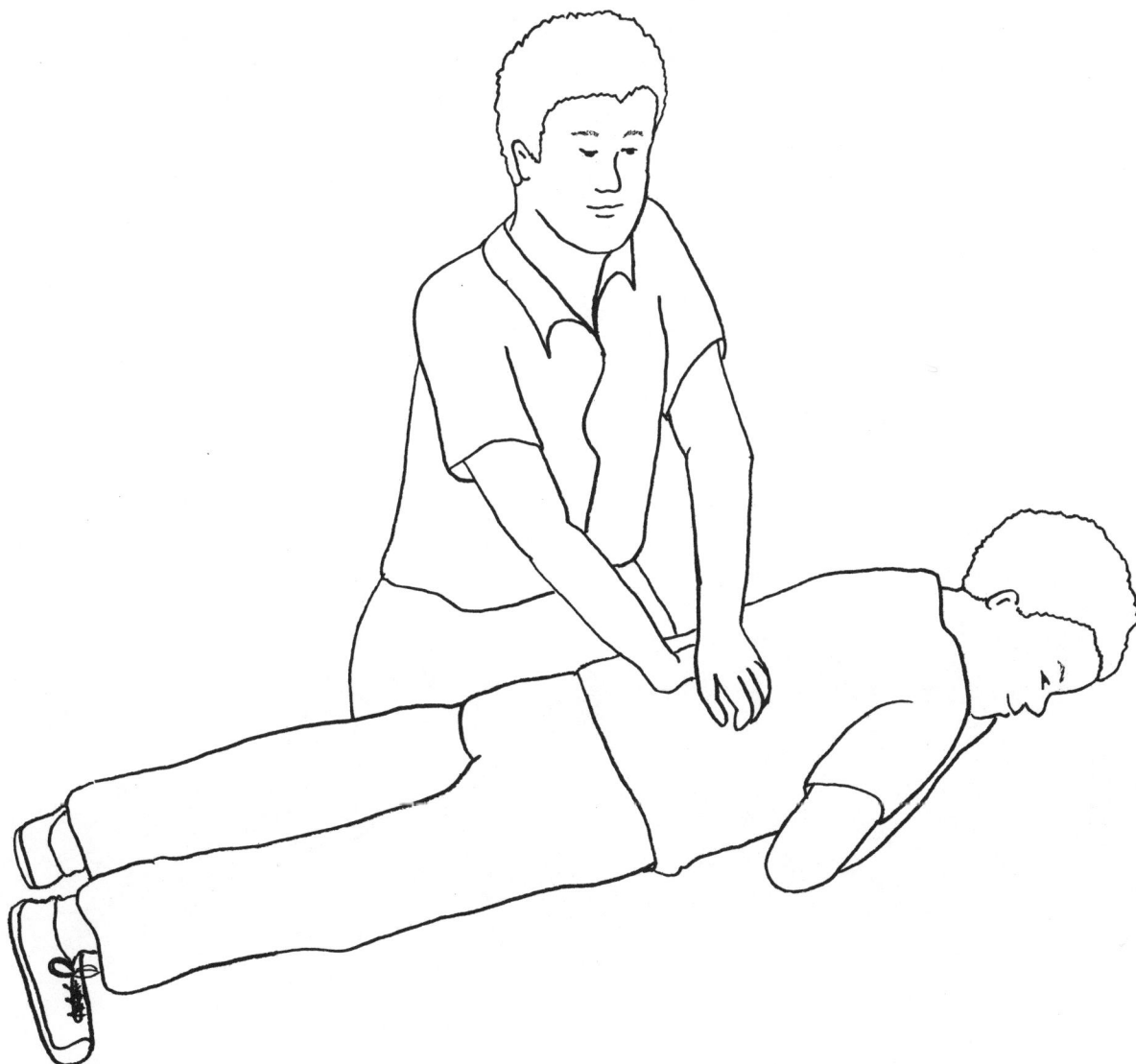

Masturbation

You can probably think of lots of ways to touch your body so that you will feel good. When you feel good because you touch your clitoris or vagina, or penis or testicles, this is called *masturbation*.

Sometimes when boys touch their penis or it rubs against something it will get stiff. When boys masturbate, it feels good. Semen and sperm spurt out of the end of their penis. This spurting out is called *ejaculation*, and this good feeling is called *orgasm*. After a boy or man ejaculates, his penis gets soft again.

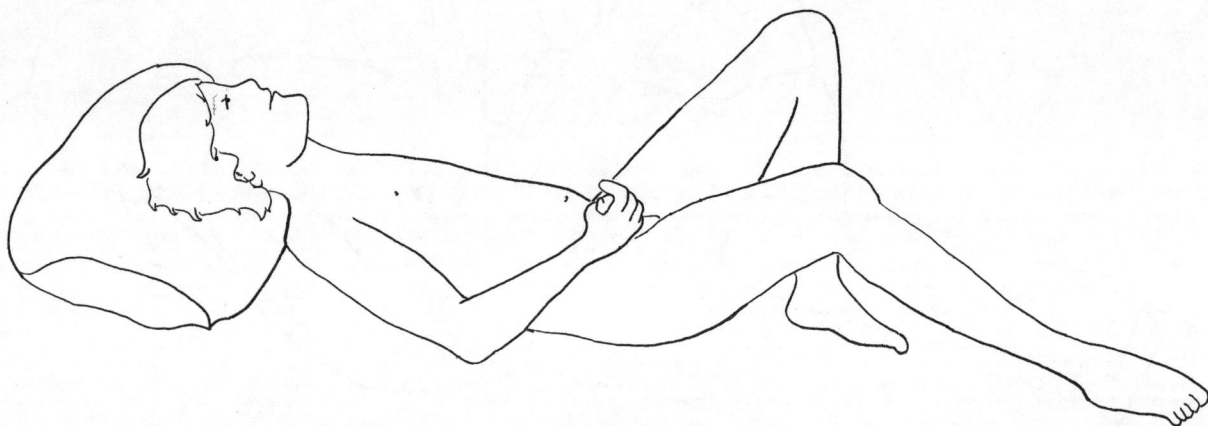

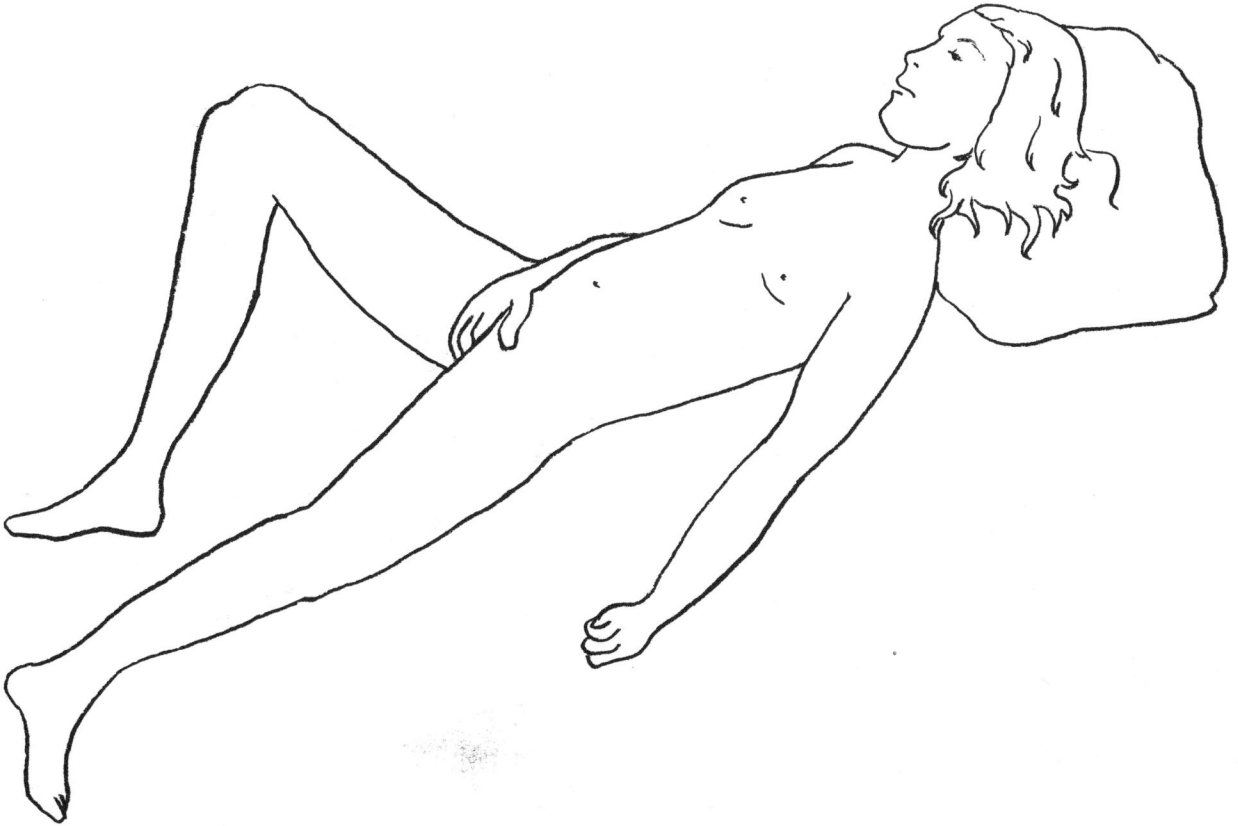

Sometimes when girls rub their clitoris or their vagina, this feels good. The vagina may become wet. This wetness is called *lubrication*. Sometimes their clitoris will get hard. This is also an erection. Girls do not ejaculate, but they do have orgasms.

Masturbation is a normal, enjoyable, and healthy activity that has no bad effects. Because it feels good, almost everybody masturbates—young kids, teenagers, married people, unmarried people, and old people. This is a private act. And if you want to masturbate, you do it in private.

Dreams

Dreams are things that you think about while you sleep. Sometimes you have daydreams. Daydreams, called *fantasies*, are things you think about to make yourself feel good when you are not asleep. Everybody does this.

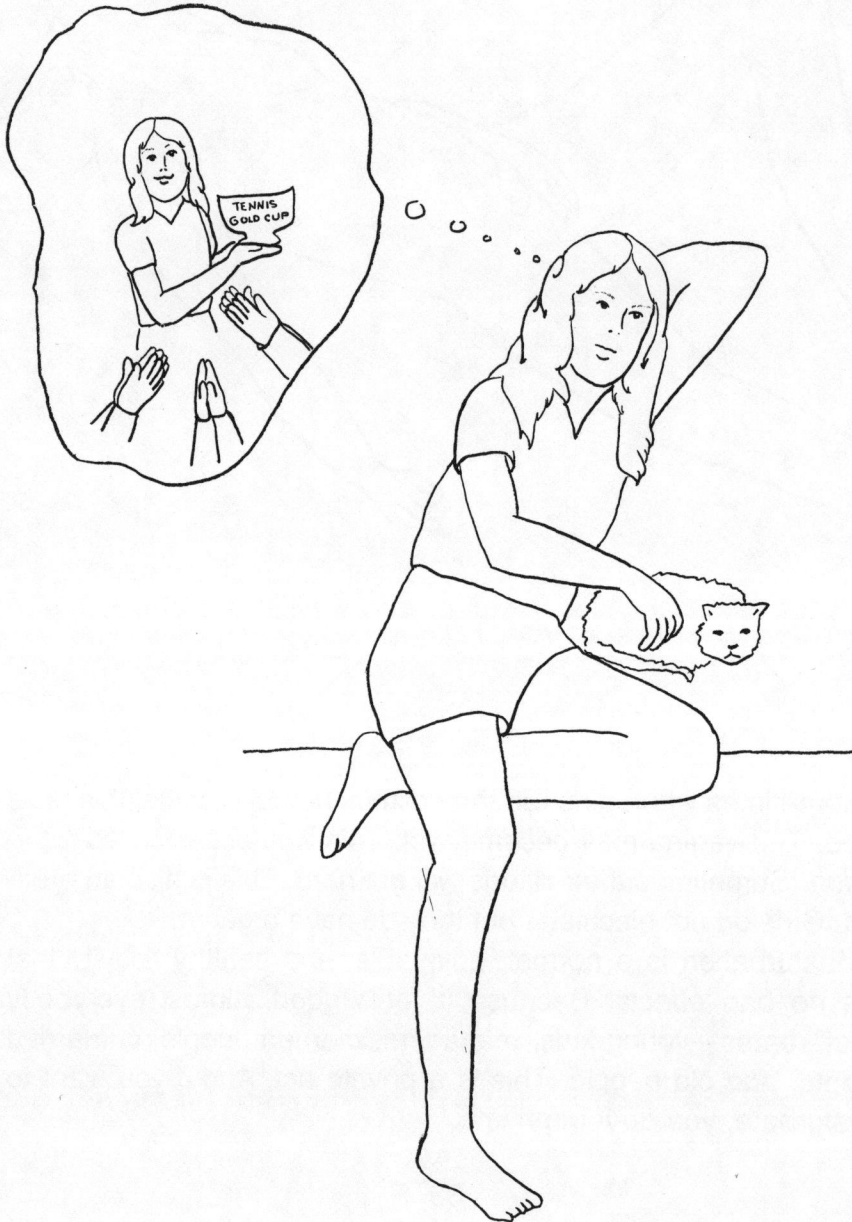

You may have *wet dreams*. Both girls and boys can have wet dreams. If you are a boy you may wake up and notice a spot on the sheets where your semen and sperm came out while you slept.

If you are a girl, you may wake up and remember a dream that made you feel good and you may notice that your vagina is wet. Even though there are no spots on the sheets, you had a wet dream.

Feelings

Feelings are an important part of life. There are all sorts of feelings. But it is sometimes hard to talk about our feelings to other people.

People have different feelings for different kinds of people. You have certain feelings for the members of your family. They are your relatives.

When you choose to play with someone or to go to the movies, to ball games, or for walks with that particular person, it is because you like being with him or her—you are friends.

Sometimes you may show how you feel about someone by hugging or kissing that person. You have received a hug or kiss from your mother or father or someone else. This is because of the way they feel about you.

We even hug our pets sometimes.

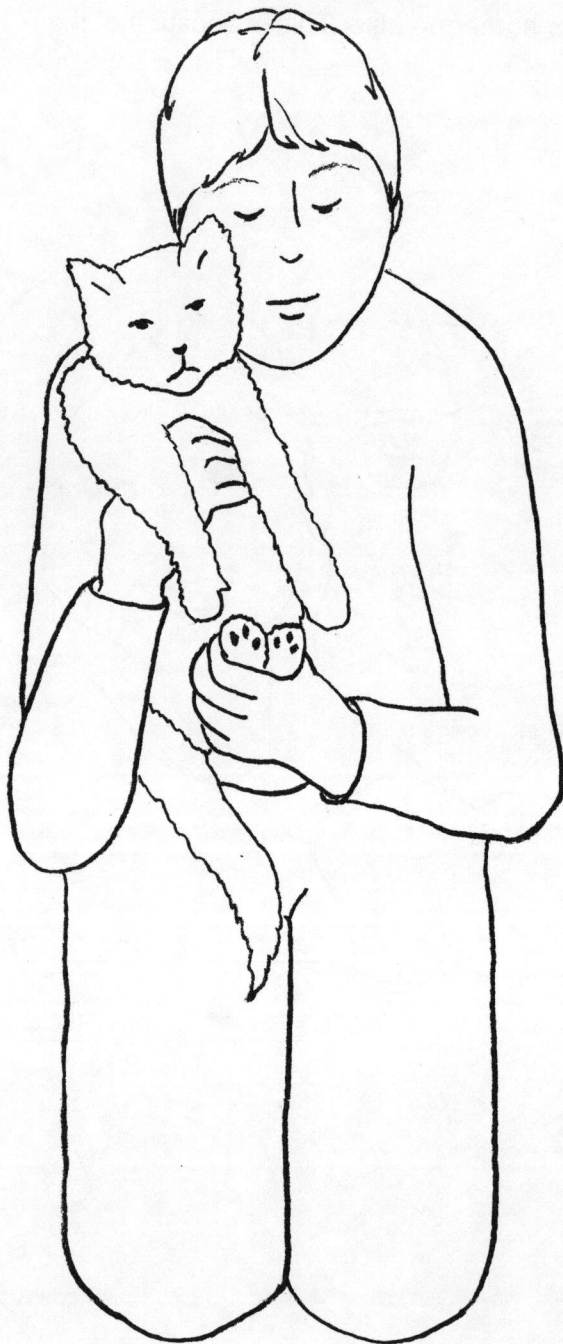

People who are married to each other have a special relation-ship. They chose to get married because they loved one another in a special way. If you like someone a little bit, that is a different type of relationship than if you love the person.

Feelings are not always good ones. We sometimes feel sad or unhappy. Even though we like our friends, we may still get mad at them once in a while. We sometimes become angry with our parents, too. But we still love them and know that they love us. Did your mother and father ever feel this way when they were your age?

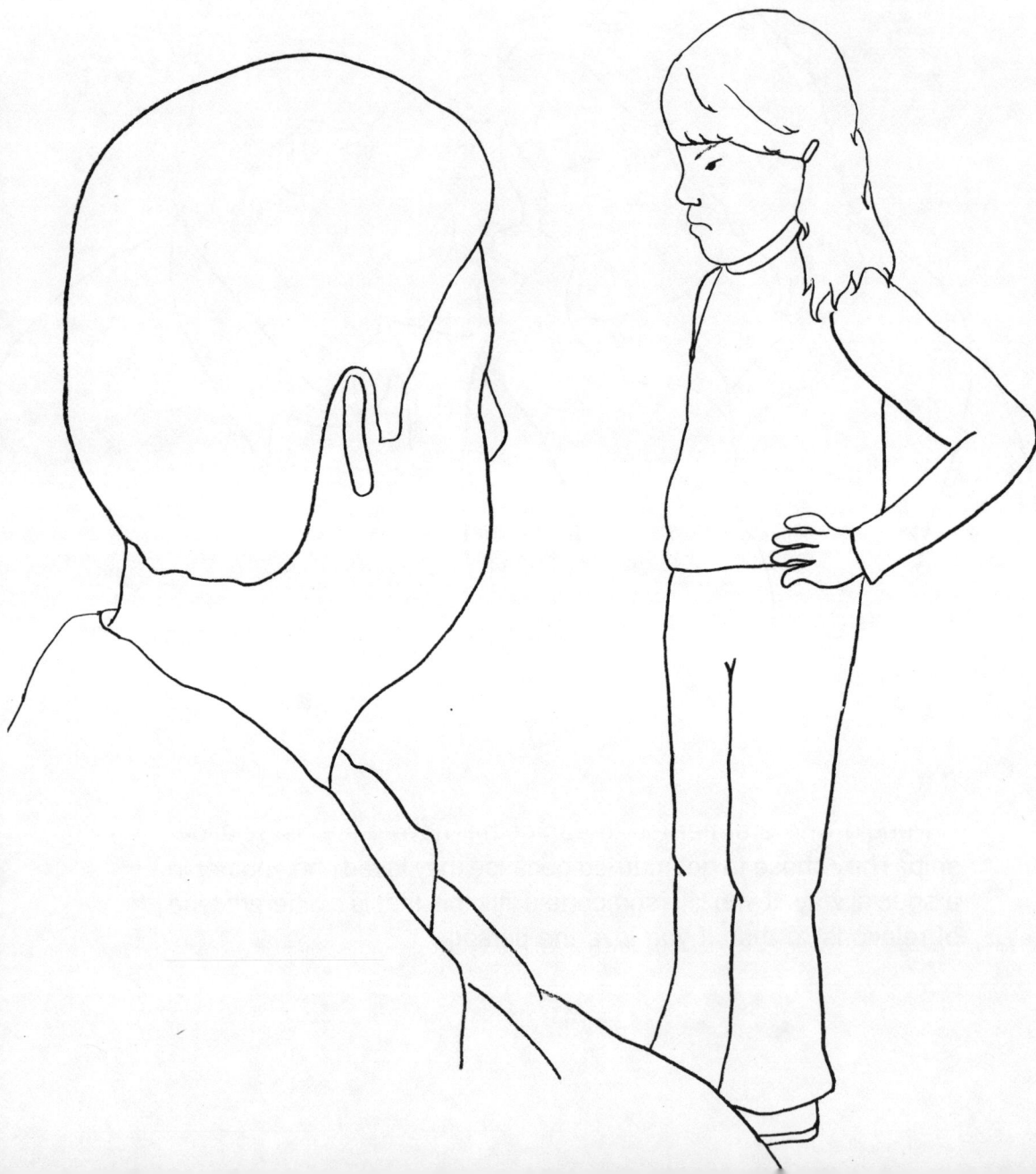

As we grow up, we begin to experience some new feelings. We don't always understand why. This is natural and normal. Just remember that you are like everybody else who grew up. We all have different feelings at different times.

If you feel a certain way and it bothers you because you can't understand why you feel that way, talk to your father or mother about it. Mothers and fathers were once children too.

As you get older, you will learn more about your own and other people's feelings. Just like the rest of you, your feelings will grow up too.

Feelings are also an important part of sex. Some adults who are in a close relationship and love one another may decide to have *sexual intercourse* to show how much they love one another.

Husbands and wives enjoy sexual intercourse together, and so do some other adults who have a close relationship and love one another.

Sexual Intercourse

Sexual intercourse is one very special way people enjoy sex with one another. After a man and woman kiss and hug each other a lot, they may want to have sexual intercourse.

If they do, the woman spreads her legs and the man puts his erect penis into her vagina. Because of lubrication, the woman's vagina is slippery and the man's penis slides in easily. They hold each other close and the vagina and penis rub together. This feels good for both of them. As you know, sometimes when people masturbate they have an orgasm. When a man and woman touch

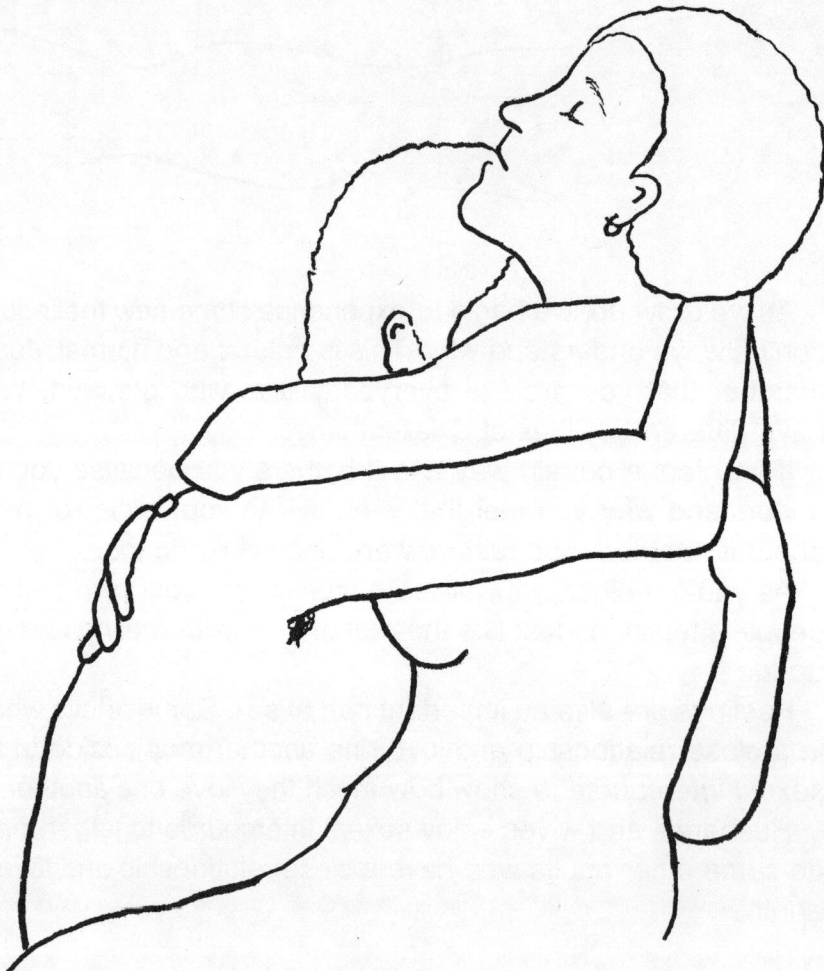

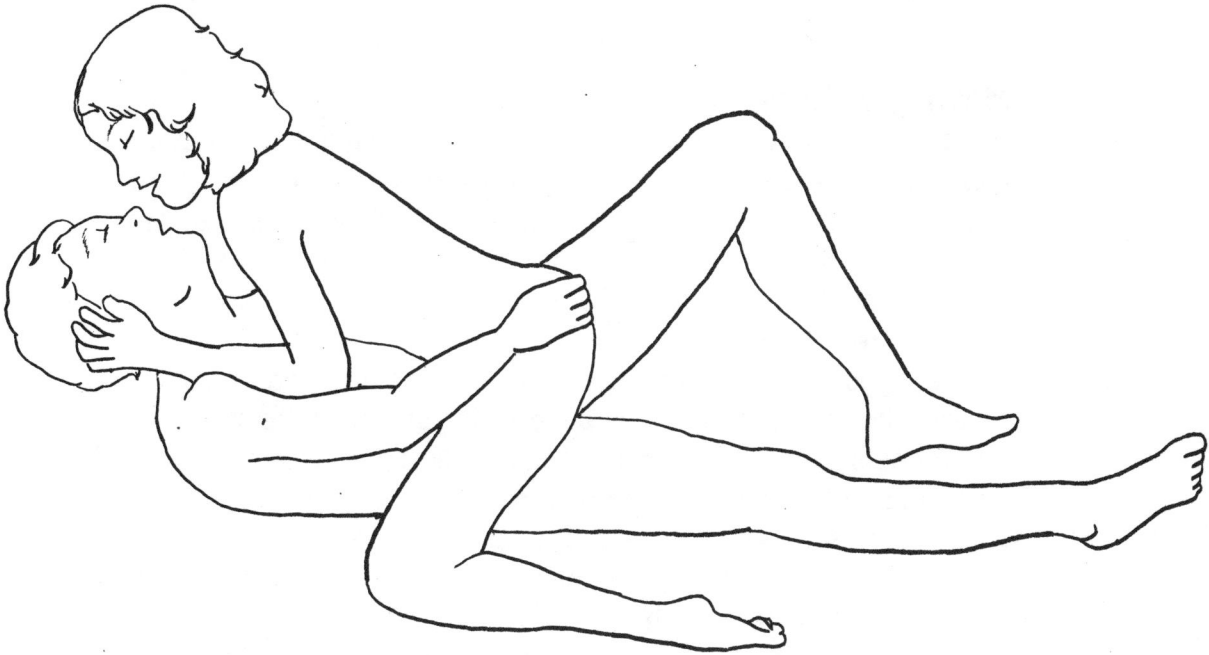

each other in a sexual way or have sexual intercourse, they can have an orgasm. Sometimes intercourse is called making love. It is very special and is done when we are grown up, with a person we love. It is a part of feelings that we have for that person. People who have intercourse must be old enough to understand their feelings, because intercourse is the one way to begin a baby. The part about feelings is hard to understand now, but you will understand this better as you get older. For now, we want you to understand that sexual intercourse means that a man moves his penis inside a woman's vagina.

People have intercourse for many reasons, but most of the time they do it because it feels good, or because they love one another and want to have a baby.

Having a Baby

Suppose a man and a woman decide they would like to have a baby. As you know, if a woman is going to become *pregnant* (have a baby growing inside her), she and the man must have sexual intercourse so that the man's sperm can join with one of the woman's eggs. Sperm is in the man's semen and is made in his testicles, remember?

The eggs in a woman's body are called *ova* (one egg is an *ovum*). Human eggs are not like the eggs you see in the store or in birds' nests—they do not have shells. Human eggs are so small you can barely see them without a microscope. All of the eggs that a woman has in her body are there from the time she is born.

A woman's eggs come from her two *ovaries*, which are inside her body. From the time that a woman reaches the age when she begins to menstruate until she reaches menopause, usually one egg will leave one of her ovaries each month.

The egg usually pops out of the ovary in the middle of her monthly menstrual cycle, which takes about twenty-eight days. This means that the egg comes out about two weeks before she menstruates. When the egg leaves the woman's ovary, it travels into one of her *fallopian tubes*. Usually one egg pops out. Sometimes more than one egg will pop out. In order for a woman's egg to grow into a baby, it must be *fertilized*—something must be added to make it grow. The only thing that will fertilize an egg in a woman is the sperm from a man.

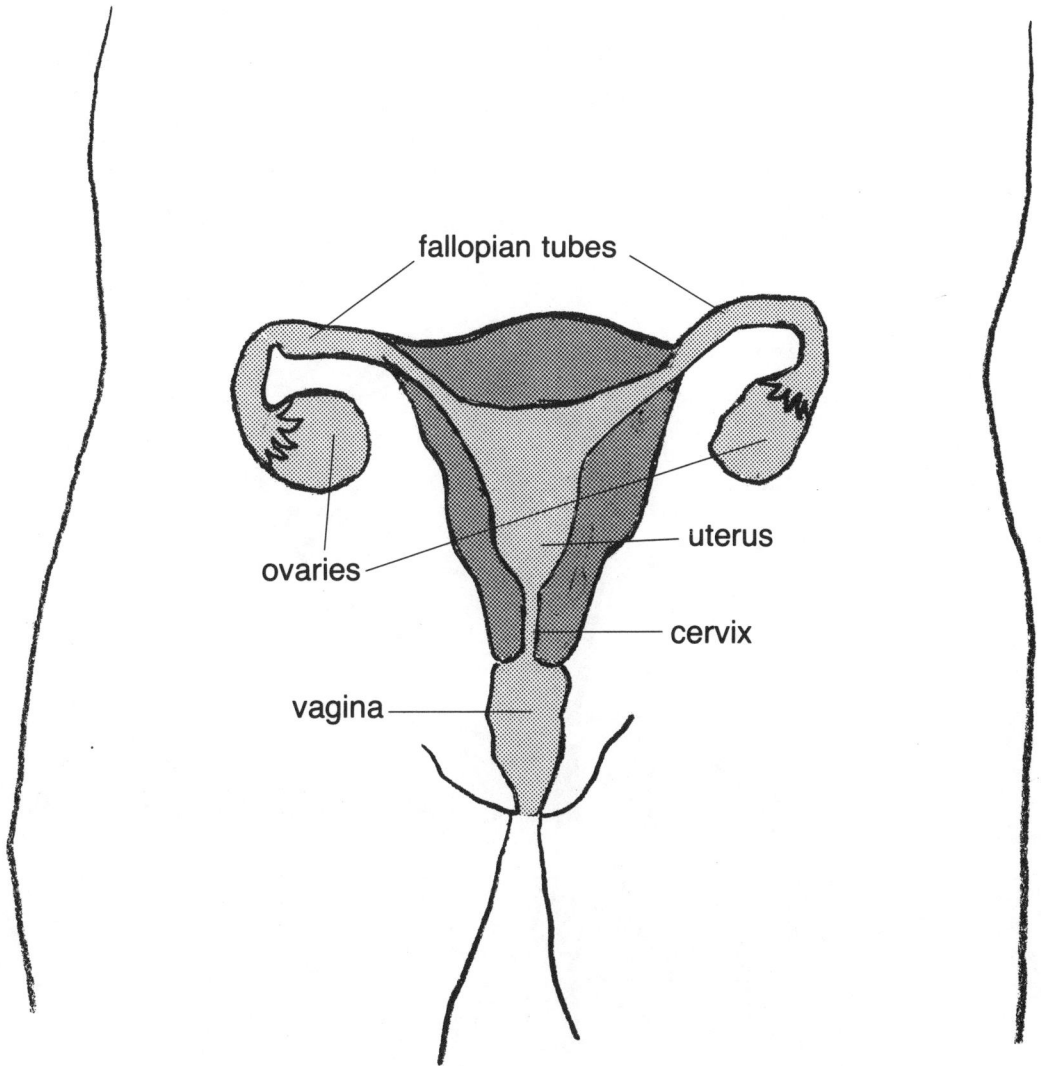

Female Reproductive Organs Inside the Body

Each time a man ejaculates, there are hundreds of millions of sperm in his semen. Sperm are very small—much smaller even than a woman's egg. It takes only one sperm to fertilize an egg. Sperm have little tails that push them toward the egg. Under a microscope, they look like little fish swimming. When the sperm are ejaculated into the woman's vagina, they swim into the *uterus* and then into the fallopian tubes.

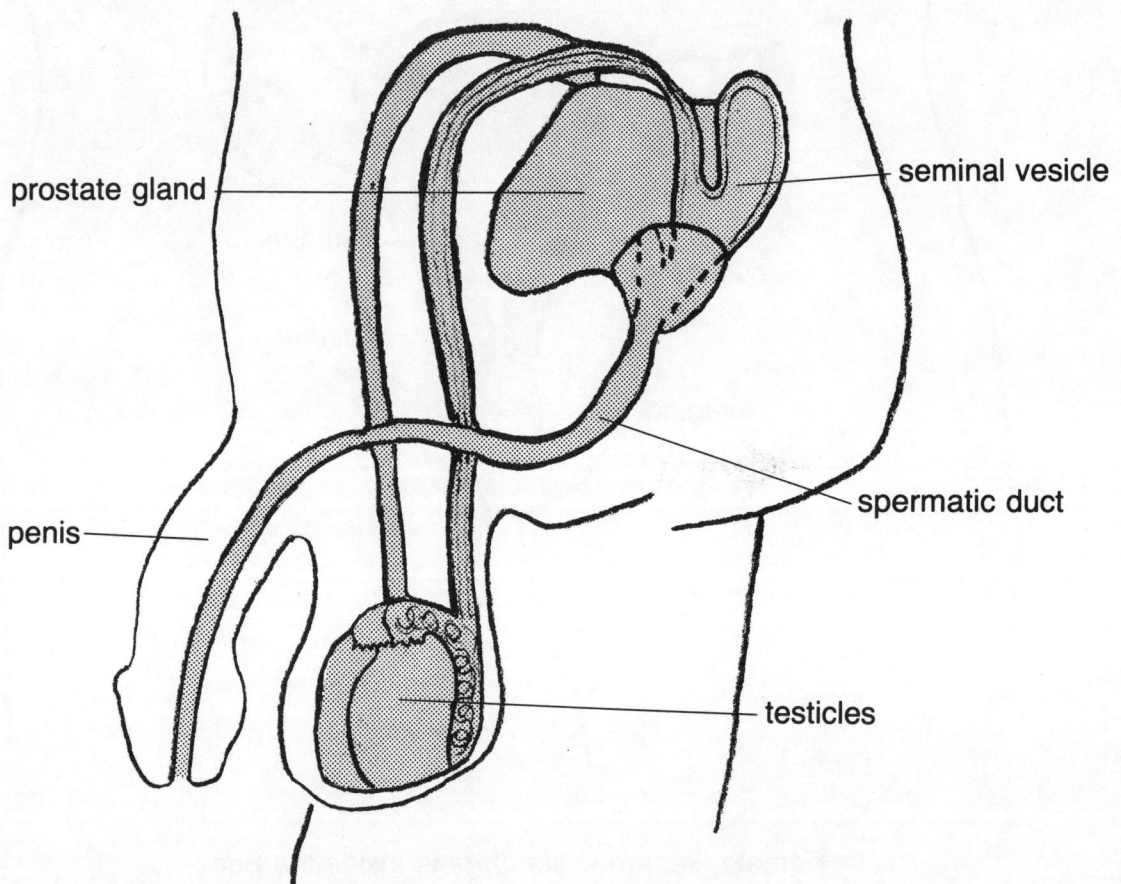

Male Reproductive Organs Inside the Body

ovum (egg)

sperm

penis in vagina

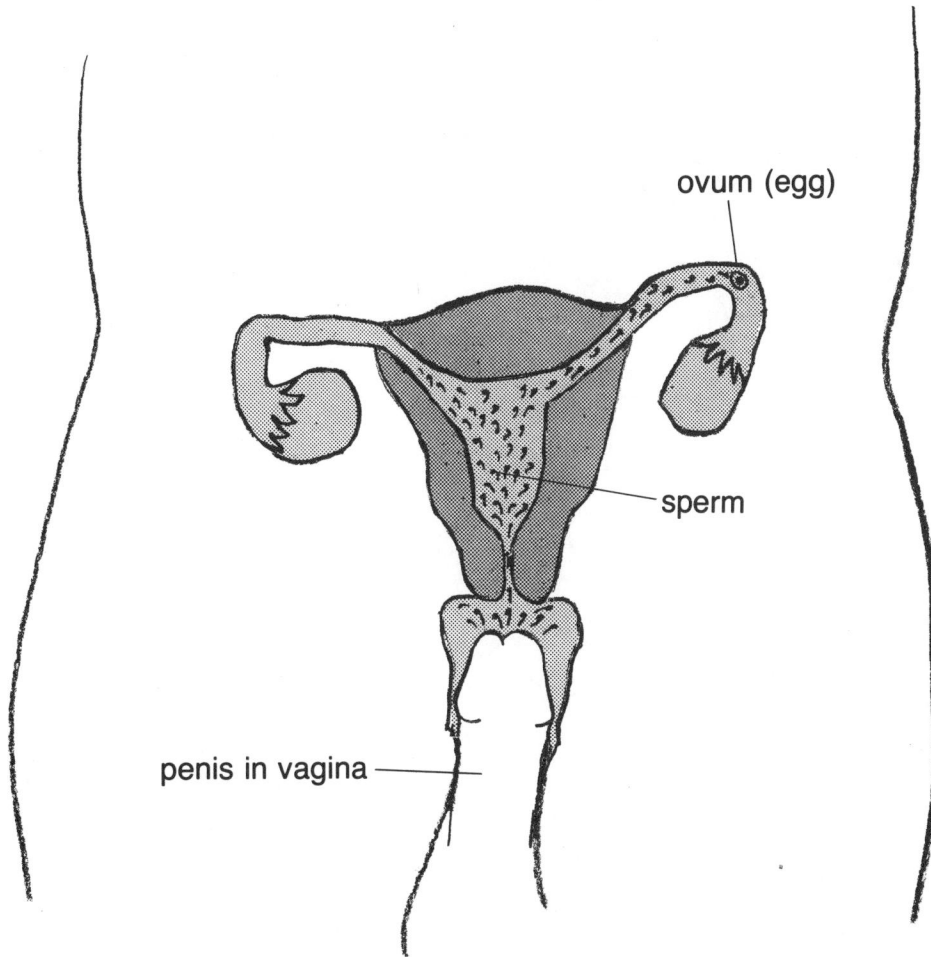

How an Egg is Fertilized

When a sperm meets the egg, the egg is fertilized and begins to
grow into a baby. If two sperm meet two eggs, there will be twins. If
this happens, the babies that grow will not look exactly alike. But if
one fertilized egg divides into two parts, the babies will be identical
twins. They will look exactly alike.

All men have two types of sperm—X and Y.

If you are a girl, it is because one of your father's X-type sperm
reached your mother's egg first.

If you are a boy, it is because one of your father's Y-type sperm
reached your mother's egg before the X-type could.

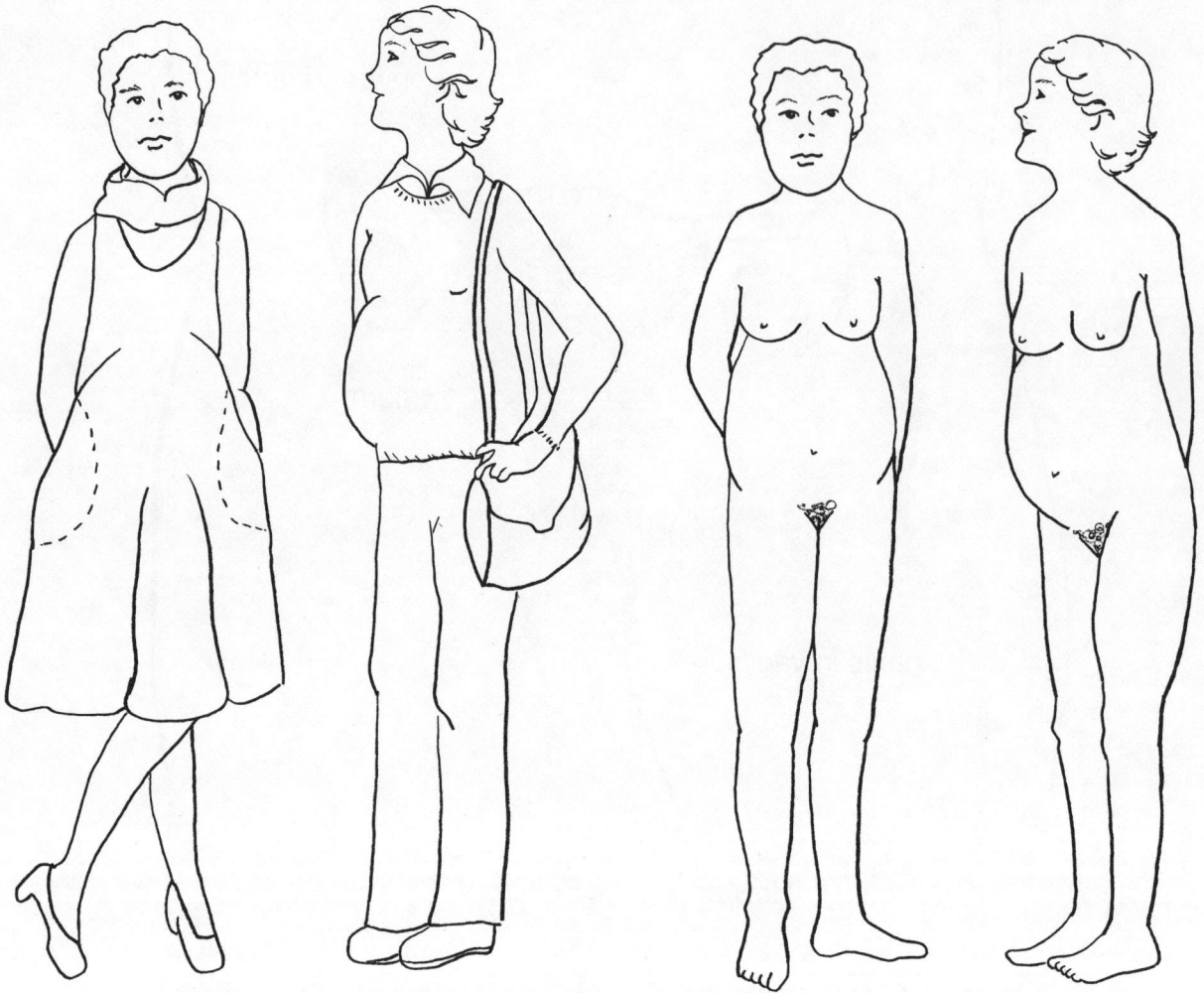

Pregnancy

A woman can tell from her menstrual period whether or not she is pregnant, because if she is pregnant, her periods will stop until the baby is born. Periods can also stop for other reasons, sometimes if the woman has been sick. But, if a man's sperm got into her vagina and moved into her fallopian tubes, she is probably pregnant. It is possible for a man's sperm to fertilize the woman's egg if he ejaculates very close to the opening of her vagina. But, usually, if a woman has not had sexual intercourse, she *cannot* be pregnant.

After an egg is fertilized in the woman's fallopian tube, it moves into her uterus. Here the baby will grow until he or she is ready to be born about nine months later. The uterus is about the size and shape of a pear. As the baby grows, the uterus also grows. After the baby is born, the uterus will shrink back to the size it was before. As long as the baby is growing inside of her uterus, a woman does not have periods, but she can still enjoy sexual inter- course.

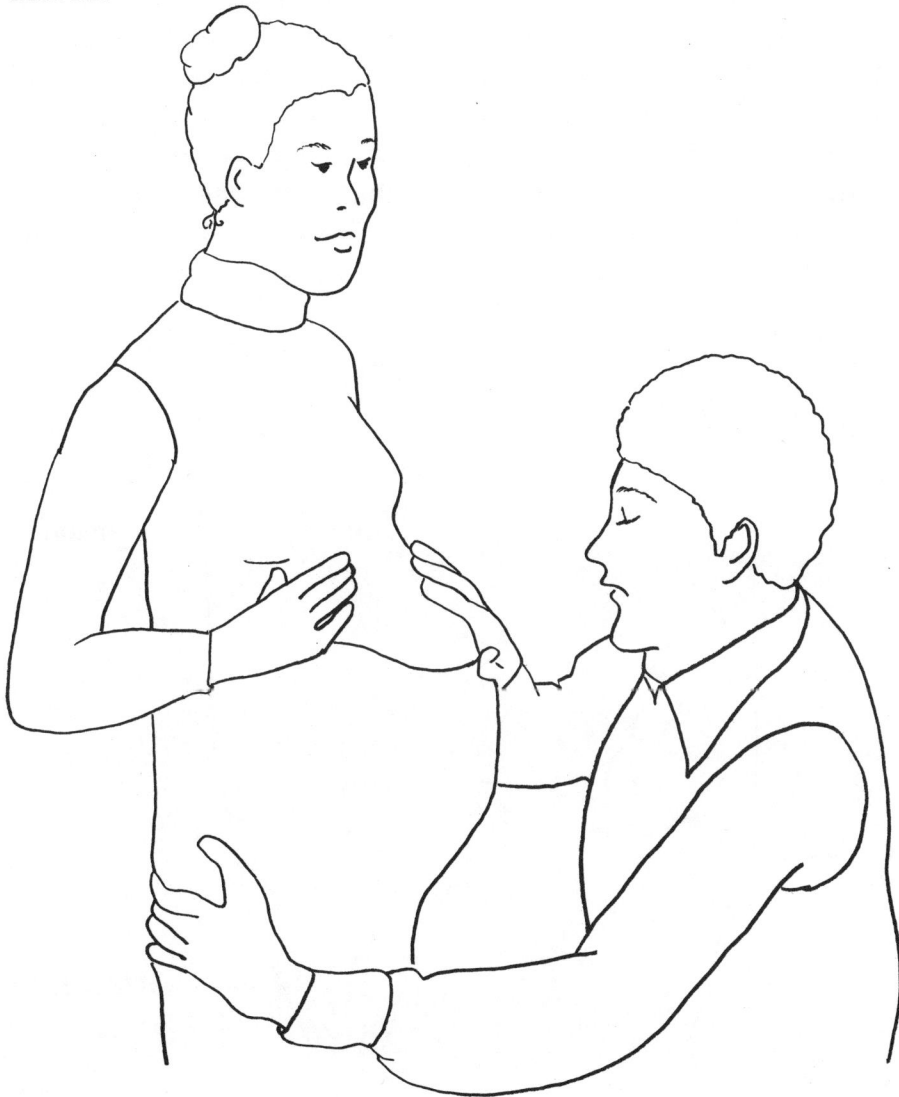

This is the way everybody in the world began. We were all smaller than the period at the end of this sentence when we began to grow inside our mothers' uterus. And look at the size of us now.

Have you ever heard stories about other ways in which babies begin? There are no other ways. Maybe when your mother or father were your age they heard other types of stories too. Ask them.

While you were growing inside of your mother's uterus, you were surrounded by a bag of liquid called *amniotic fluid*. Inside this bag, you were protected from being bumped and you were kept at a comfortable temperature. You were connected to your mother's *placenta*, which was about the size of this page. You received food from the placenta. When you were in the uterus waiting to be born, you not only needed food, you had to pee. It was such a small amount that it disappeared in the amniotic fluid.

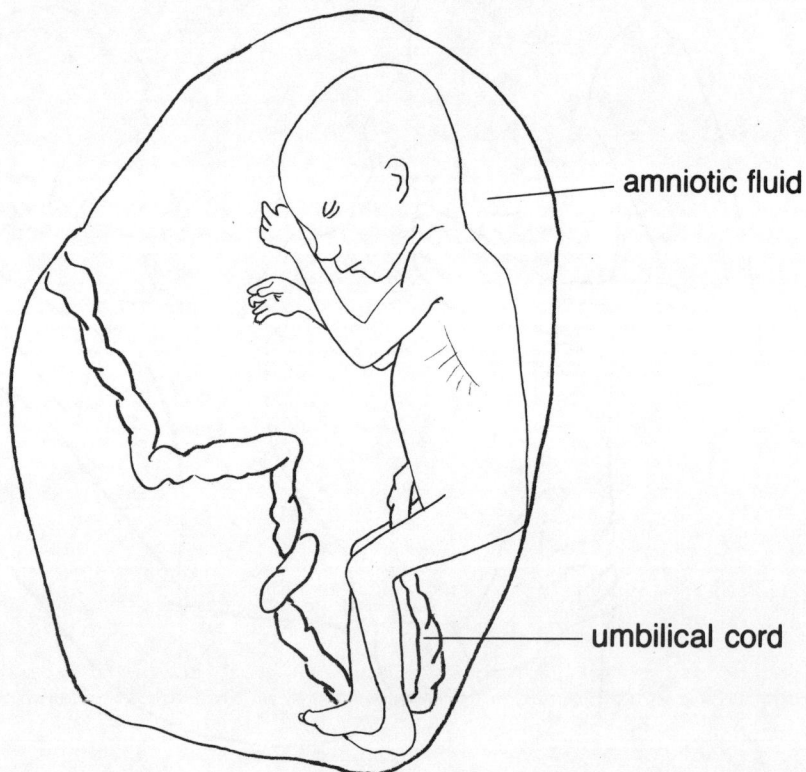

amniotic fluid

umbilical cord

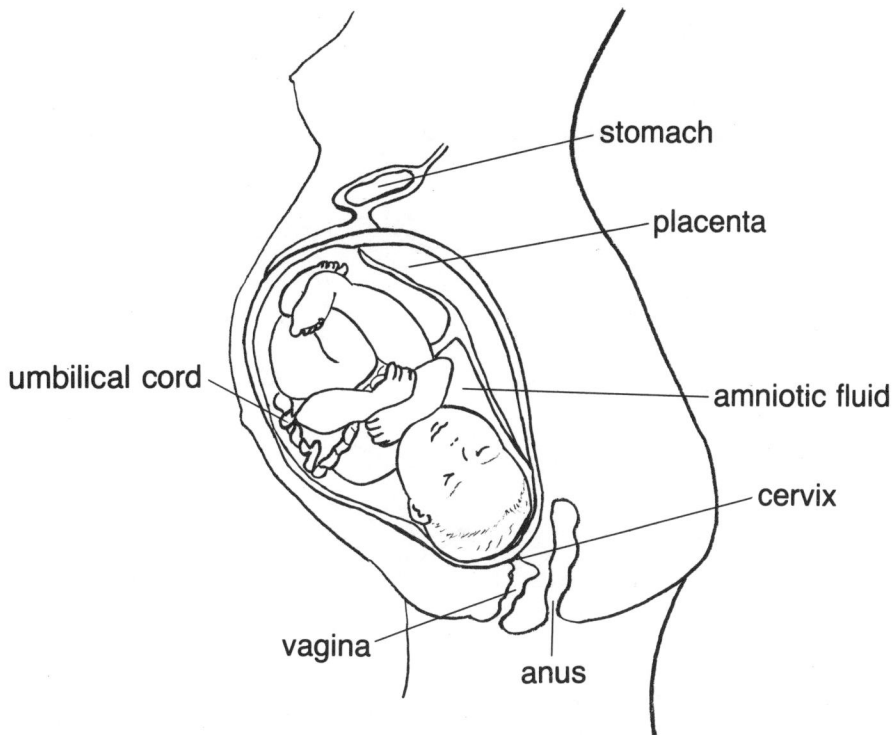

stomach
placenta
amniotic fluid
cervix
umbilical cord
vagina
anus

Everybody in the world was connected to the placenta in the same way. One thing **all** people have in common, whether they are male or female, is a belly button (*navel*). Your belly button marks the spot where you were connected to your mother's placenta by an *umbilical cord*. You received your food through the umbilical cord. When you were inside your mother's body, you didn't have to breathe. The umbilical cord kept you alive. You just floated peacefully in the amniotic fluid.

After about nine months of growing inside your mother's uterus, you were ready to be born. When you began to move from the uterus toward your mother's vagina, she began to feel slight pains around her uterus. These pains are called *contractions* because the uterus was starting to contract—to get smaller, and push you out. The bag of amniotic fluid broke and the liquid (water) ran through your mother's vagina. Not too long after that you were born.

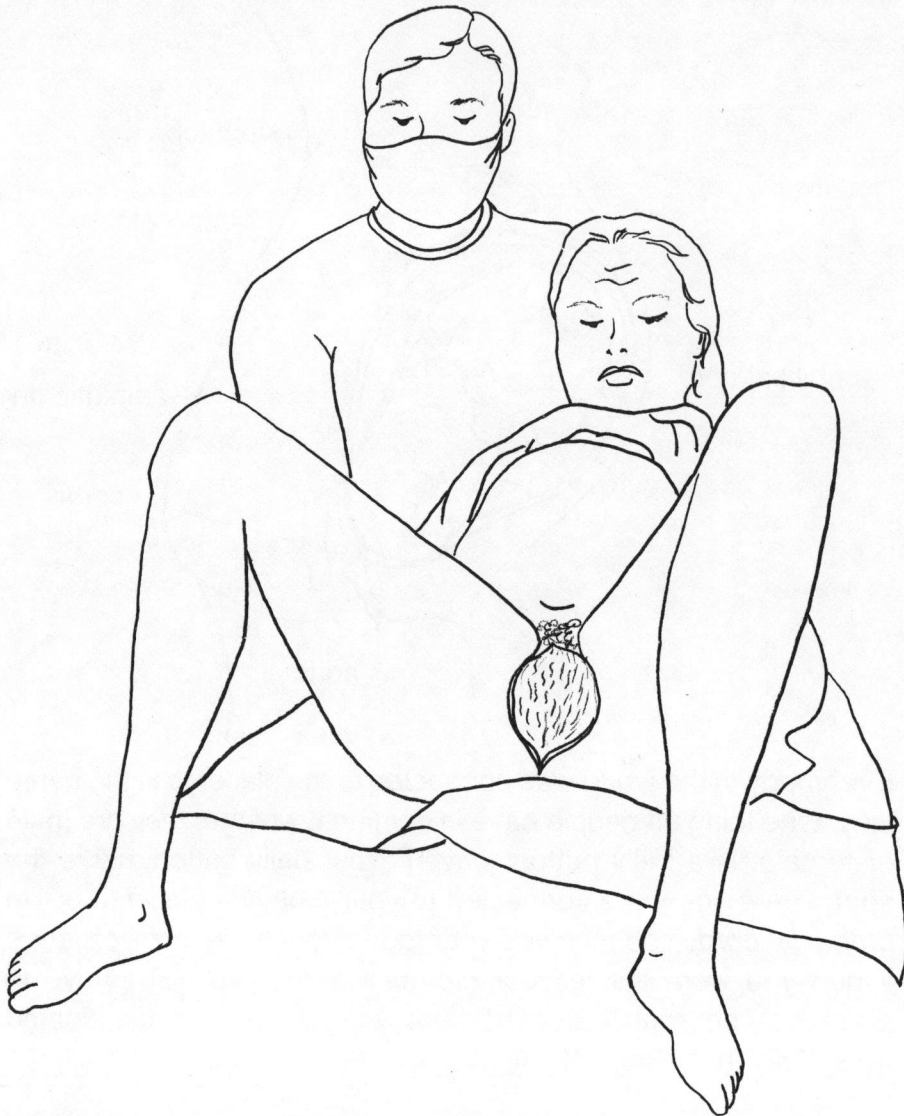

Birth

Your mother had to help push you out by using certain muscles. You may have heard the term *labor* or *being in labor*. This pushing is called labor because it involves a lot of hard work. Some mothers and fathers go to classes together before the baby is born (just like you go to school) to learn how to make the birth of the baby (the delivery) easier. Usually, the father and mother learn certain exercises which will make pushing in labor a lot easier.

At times labor hurts, but your mother wanted you so much and was so anxious to see what you looked like, that she forgot about the pain as soon as you were born.

As soon as you were born, you began to breathe. Your umbilical cord was cut and you became a separate person. Your umbilical cord had no nerves. It didn't hurt when it was cut—just like when your hair is cut.

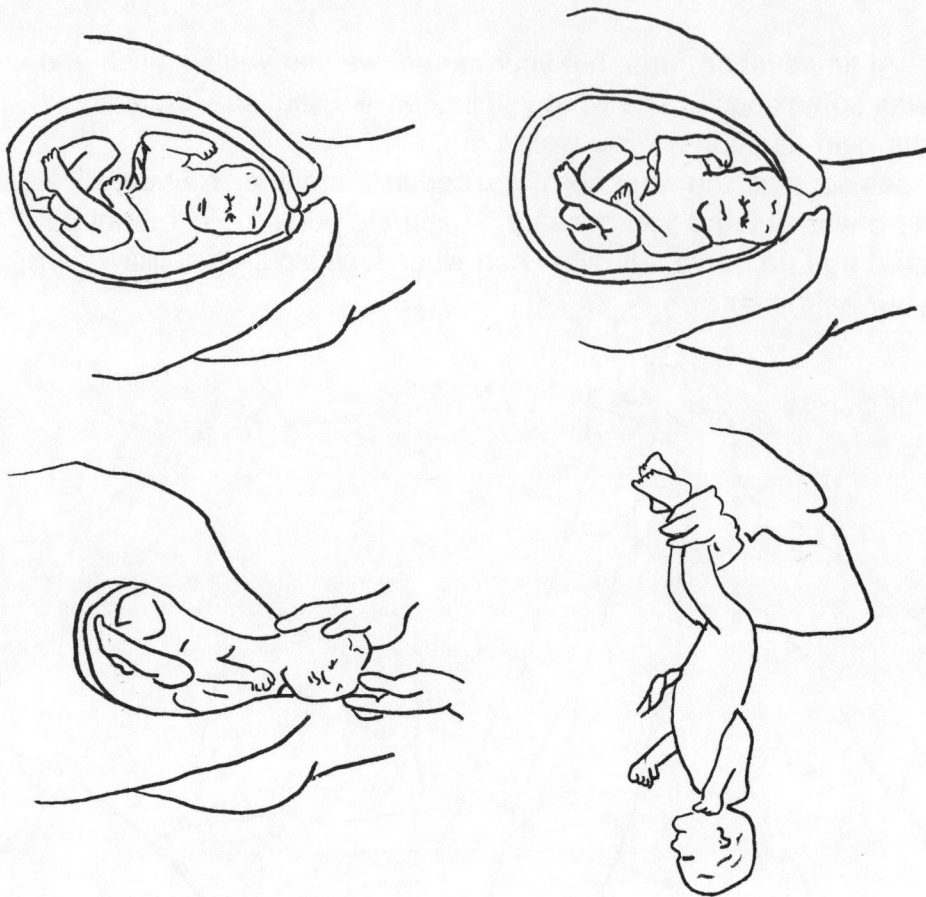

Most of the time, babies are born head first, but some babies are not. When a baby is born buttocks first, the delivery is called a *breech birth*. Were you a breech-birth baby? Other times, the doctor feels that it would be best for the baby not to be born through the mother's vagina. In that case, the baby is lifted out through a small opening the doctor makes in the mother's abdomen. This is called a *cesarean birth*. Were you a cesarean-birth baby? Sometimes a baby is born before the nine months are up and needs special care because he or she is so small. Such a baby is called a *premature baby*. Were you a premature baby? We know you can't remember any of this—so you will have to ask your mother or father.

The father may have to help the mother before and after the baby is born. Do you have any older brothers or sisters? If you do, and you were born in a hospital, your father may have had to take care of them a little more than usual just before and after you were born. Maybe you have younger brothers or sisters and your father had to spend a little more time taking care of you when they were born.

All new babies need lots of love and attention. Babies have to be fed, held, burped so they won't get a stomach ache, and have their diapers changed regularly.

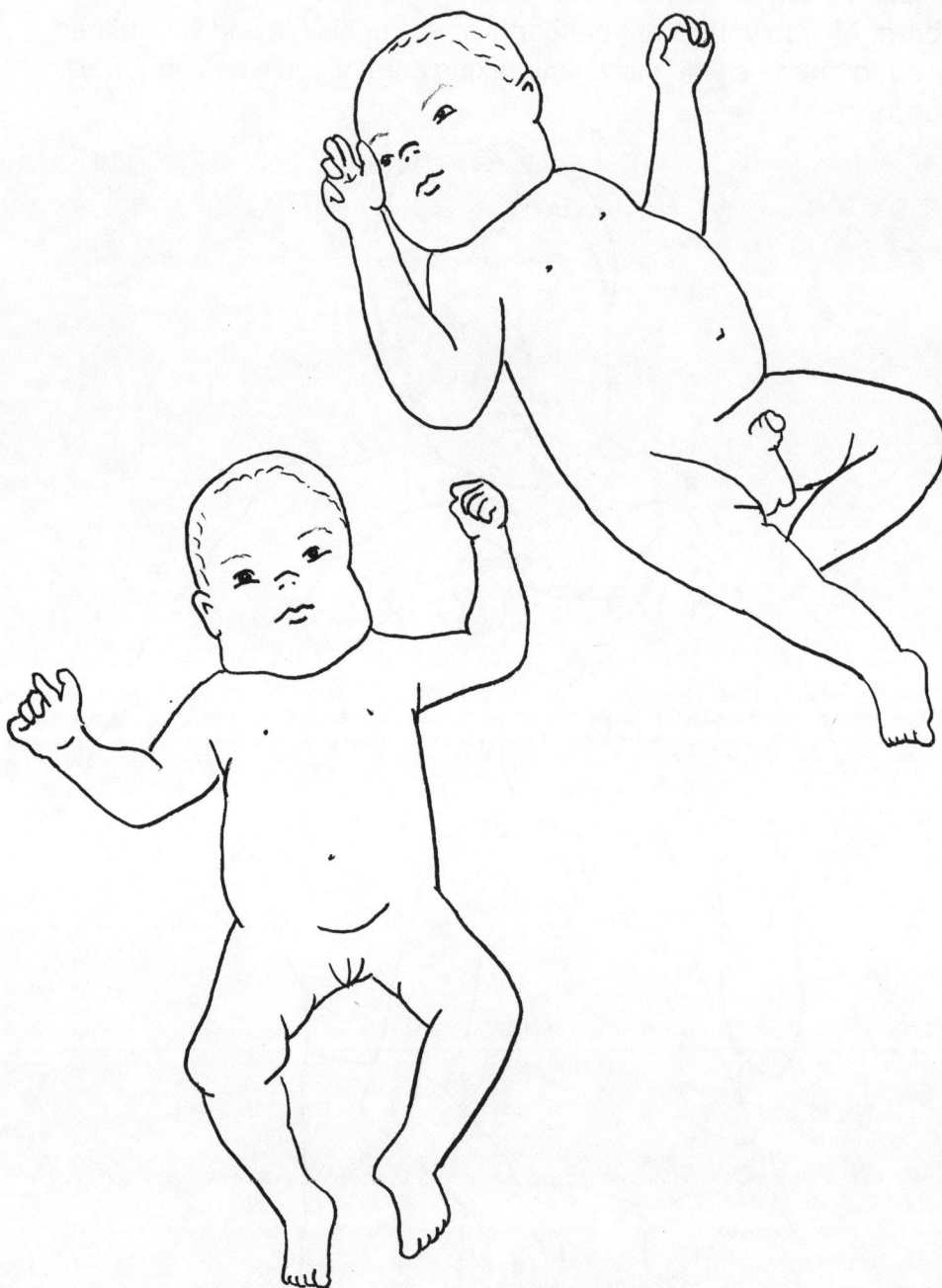

This is why before a man and a woman decide to have a baby,
they should be certain they will be able to give it all the love and
attention it will need. If babies are fed with milk from their mother's
breasts, the father can help with everything else, such as the cook-
ing, cleaning, and changing the baby's diapers. Were you breast-
fed?

Or, if the baby is fed with milk from a bottle, then the father can help feed the baby too. If your father was not there after you were born, your mother may have had someone else to help her. Or if she was by herself, she may have done everything herself. Ask your mother or father what you were like when you were a baby.

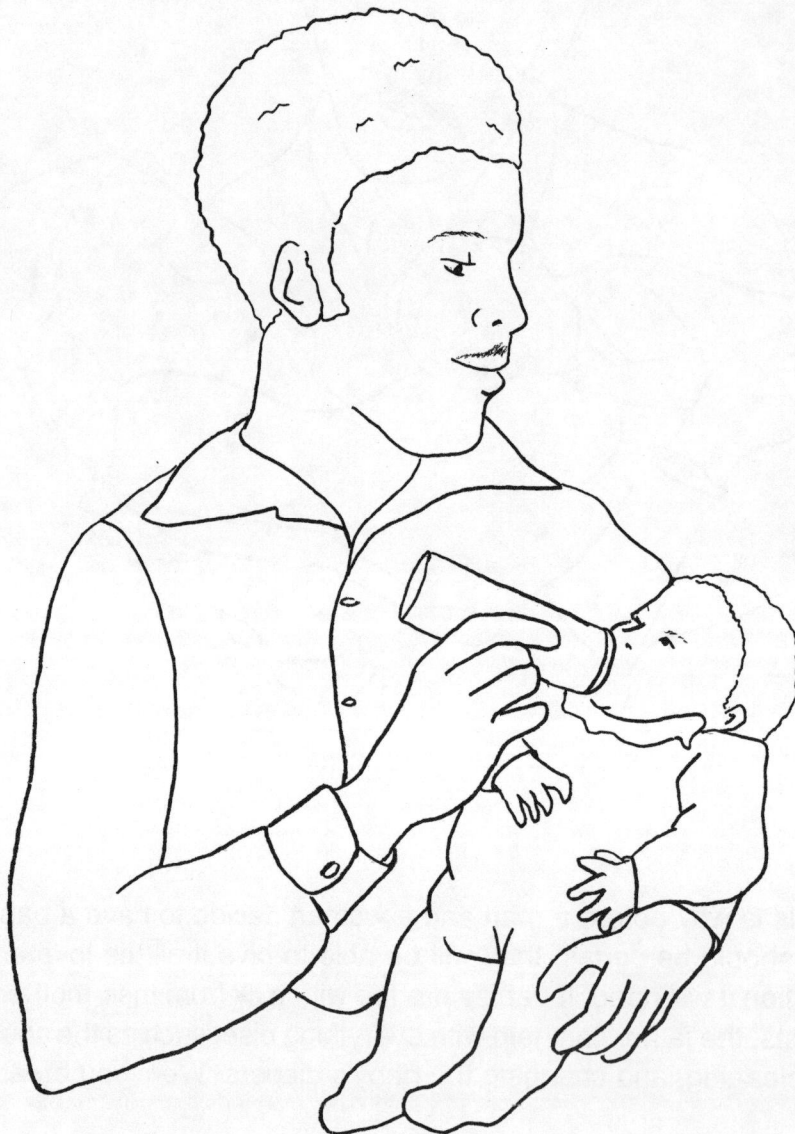

Birth Control

Most of the time when people have intercourse they do not want a baby to begin. So the man and the woman have to keep the man's sperm from meeting the egg in the woman's body. To do this, they must use *birth control*.

There are lots of different kinds of birth control. *Contraceptive foam* is squirted into the vagina with an applicator before intercourse to block the sperm from getting to the egg. Although the foam will act by itself, this form of birth control will be much more effective if the man wears a *condom* whenever the woman uses foam. We will tell you more about the condom later.

Some women would rather take a *birth control pill* every day. The pill keeps the woman's eggs from leaving her ovaries so that it is not possible for sperm to reach them. She can get these pills only with a prescription from her doctor.

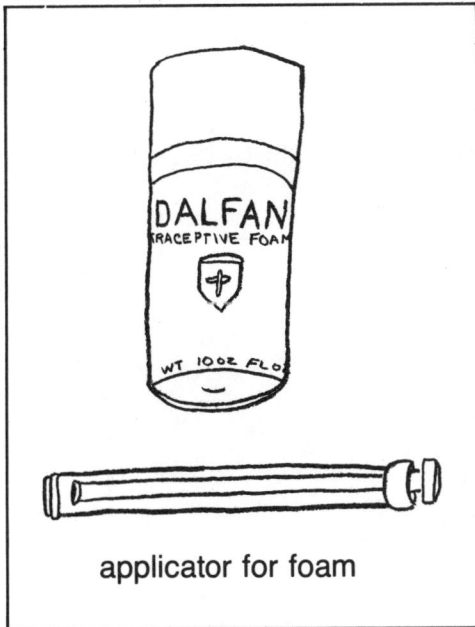

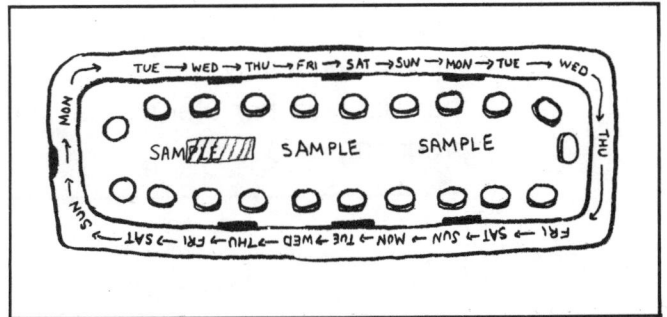

DALFAN
RACEPTIVE FOAM

WT 10 oz FL o

applicator for foam

TUE → WED → THU → FRI → SAT → SUN → MON → TUE → WED

SAMPLE   SAMPLE   SAMPLE

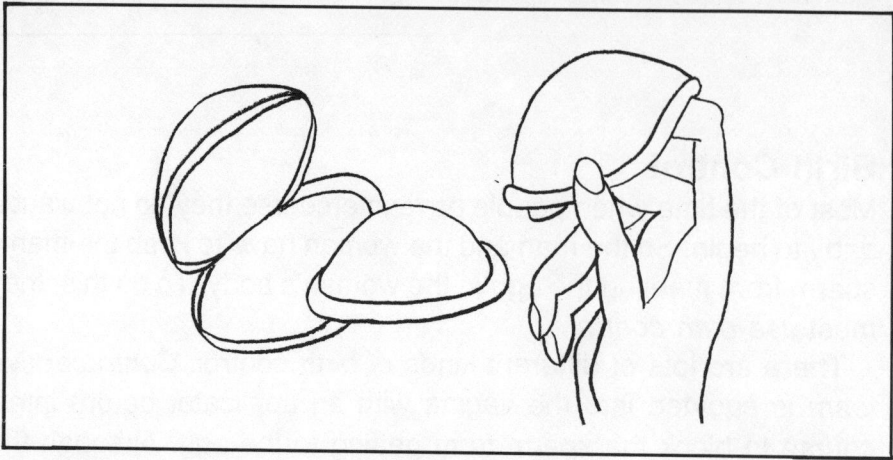

A rubber disc called a *diaphragm* is another way that a woman can block sperm from entering her uterus and meeting with her egg in the fallopian tube. The woman goes to a doctor to be measured for a diaphragm. The doctor shows her how to use it. Once she buys a diaphragm from the drugstore, she can place it in her vagina each time she plans to have intercourse. With a little practice, she will be able to do this with no trouble at all. The diaphragm covers the *cervix* (the opening to the uterus) and cannot be felt by the man's penis during intercourse.

A woman must also see a doctor if she wants to have an *IUD* (I-U-D) put in her uterus. The doctor puts the IUD in the woman's uterus, and it stays there until the doctor takes it out again. While the IUD is in her uterus, the woman will not be able to become pregnant.

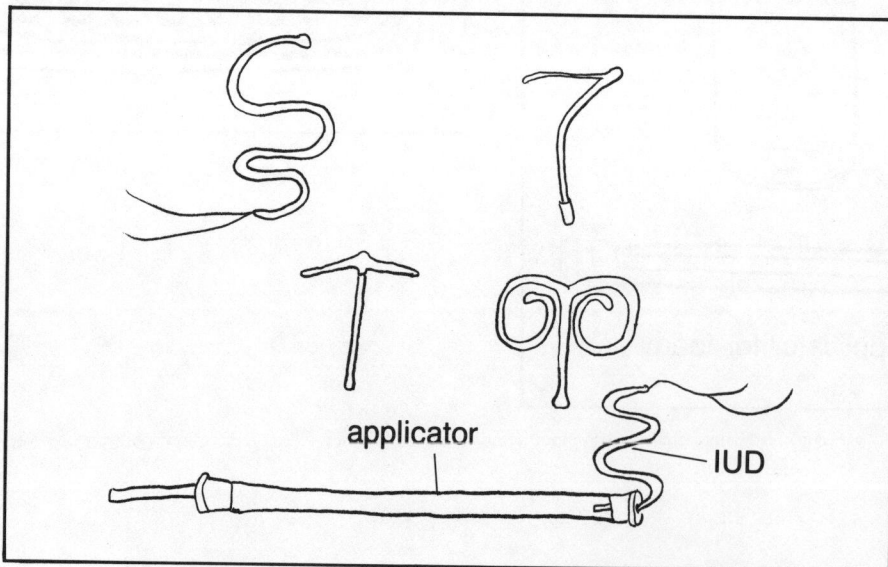

applicator

IUD

Four Kinds of IUD's and Applicator Doctor Uses

There is one thing the man can do. He can put a condom over his penis to catch the sperm so that it does not get into the woman's vagina. The condom is also called a *rubber*. It is made of rubber and looks like an empty balloon before it is placed on a stiff penis.

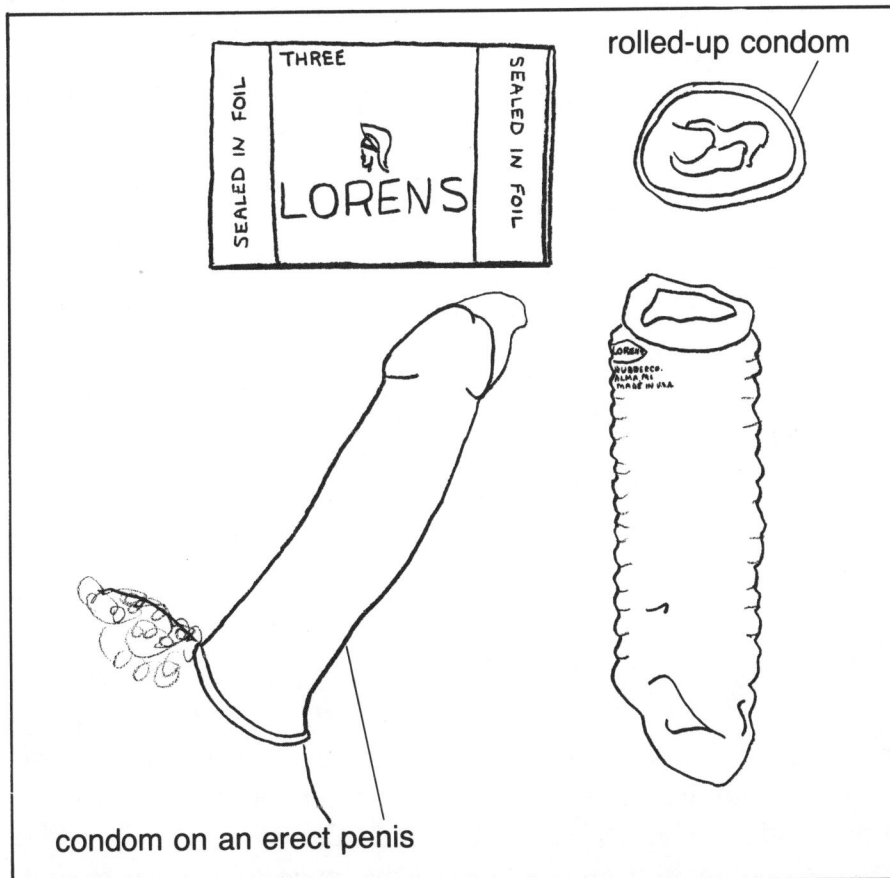

rolled-up condom

condom on an erect penis

All of these—contraceptive foams, birth control pills, diaphragms, IUDs, and condoms (rubbers)—allow men and women to enjoy sexual intercourse and not worry about the woman's becoming pregnant. When a man and woman have intercourse they should use birth control unless they are certain they want to have a baby and can give it all the love and attention it will need.

V.D.

The letters VD stand for *venereal disease*. It is a disease that people can get when they have sexual intercourse with a person who already has VD. VD is a serious disease.

Many people who have VD get it because they have sexual intercourse with a person they may not know very well who is carrying VD germs. The only way to catch VD is by having close sexual contact, such as sexual intercourse, with a person who has VD germs.

You cannot get VD from kissing or hugging, or from toilet seats. When your mother or father were growing up they probably heard a lot of untrue stories about how people get VD. Ask them.

64

VD can be cured. But a person who has VD must go to a doctor for pills and shots, or he or she can become seriously ill.

A simple way for people to keep from getting VD is to use a condom or rubber. The rubber does two good things. It keeps a woman from getting pregnant if she does not want to have a baby, and it keeps a man and a woman from getting VD from one another. Rubbers allow men and women to enjoy sexual intercourse without worrying about pregnancy or VD.

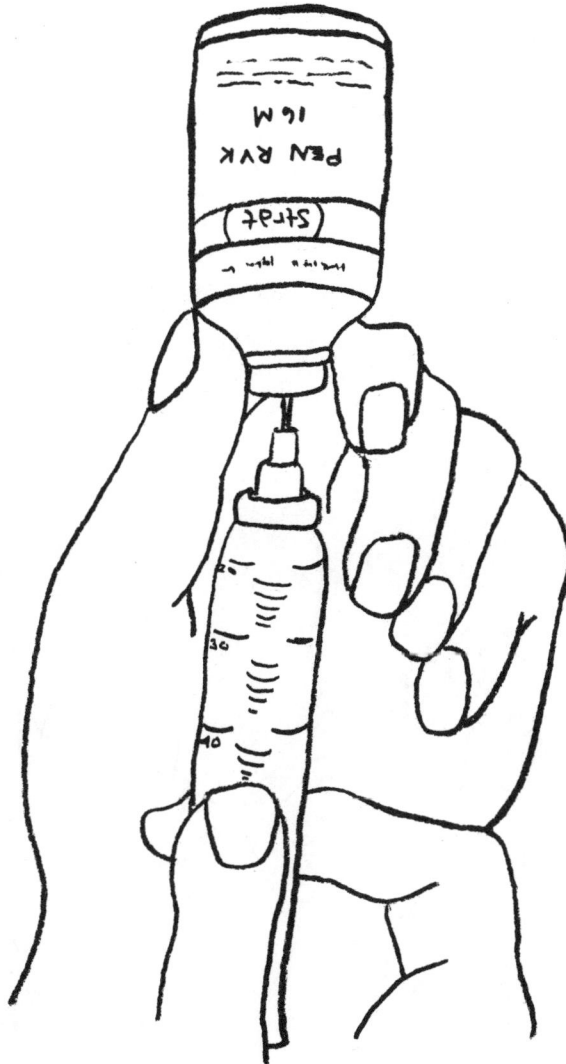

Sex Offenders

Whenever people behave in a sexual way, it must be something they both **agree** to. There are a few people who do not respect either the wishes of others, or the privacy of another person's body. These people are called *sex offenders*. Some of them take advantage of children, because children are smaller and can be forced to do what they want. Such people are called *child molesters*. Each person's body is private and deserves to be respected. It is wrong for others to look at or touch your body or try to force you to do what *they* want.

In many schools, maybe yours, you are warned not to go with strangers. The reason for this is that since you do not know who a stranger is, you can never know why this person wants you to go with him or her. Although the person may be nice to you at first, later on you might be hurt if you do not do what he or she wants you to do.

Fortunately, there are only a few sex offenders. Most likely, you and your friends will never meet one. But it is important to know what you should do if you ever meet such a person. If a person wants you to go somewhere, or offers you money or a present if you will—DON'T GO! Act like a detective, think hard about what the person looks like, and tell your parents or teacher all about it immediately.

All Human Beings Are Sexual Beings

Now you can see that sex is a natural and normal part of being human. You know the ways in which males and females are alike and the ways in which they are different. You have learned something about feelings as well as about sex. As you continue to grow, you will think of other questions. Never be afraid to ask your parents what they think. Your parents had the same types of questions when they were your age. You probably have heard that kids cannot talk to their parents about these things. But lots of times, kids don't give their parents the chance to. Give your parents the chance to let you know what they think. If that is impossible for one reason or another, talk to an older relative or close friend that you feel comfortable with and that you respect.

Word List

Word we use in the book
The word you probably hear

ANUS
Asshole

Word we use in the book
Some words you probably hear

BREASTS
Boobs
Jugs
Knockers
Tits

Word we use in the book
Some words you probably hear

BUTTOCKS
Ass
Butt

Word we use in the book
The word you probably hear

CLITORIS
Clit

Word we use in the book
Some terms you probably hear

EJACULATE
Come
Shoot Your Wad

Word we use in the book
Some words you probably hear

ERECTION
Boner
Hard-on

Word we use in the book
Some terms you probably hear

MASTURBATION
Beating Off
Jerking Off
Rubbing Off
Whacking Off

Word we use in the book   MENOPAUSE
What you probably hear   Go Through the Change

Word we use in the book   MENSTRUATION
What you probably hear   To Be on the Rag
To Be Having a Period

Word we use in the book   ORGASM
What you probably hear   To Come

Word we use in the book   PENIS
Some words you probably hear   Cock
Dick
Dink
Peter

Word we use in the book   PREGNANT
Some terms you probably hear   Expecting
Having a Baby
To Be Knocked Up

Term we use in the book   SANITARY NAPKIN
Some words you probably hear   Kotex
Rag

Term we use in the book   SEMEN AND SPERM
Some words you probably hear   Come
Pud
Wad

Term we use in the book   SEXUAL INTERCOURSE
Some terms you probably hear   Balling
Banging
Doing It
Fucking
Going All the Way
Laying
Screwing
Shooting a Load

Word we use in the book	TAMPON
The word you probably hear	Tampax
Word we use in the book	TESTICLES
Some words you probably hear	Balls
	Nuts
Word we use in the book	VAGINA
Some words you probably hear	Beaver
	Cunt
	Pussy
	Snatch
	Twat
Term we use in the book	VENEREAL DISEASE (VD)
Some words you probably hear	Clap
	Dose
	Social Disease
	Syph
Term we use in the book	WET DREAM
Term you probably hear	To Starch the Sheets

Glossary

Amniotic fluid: The liquid inside a pregnant woman's uterus where her unborn baby floats.

Anus: The opening in the body where poop comes out.

Birth Control: Ways to keep a woman from getting pregnant.

Birth Control Pill: A pill taken every day which stops a woman's eggs from leaving her ovaries so she cannot become pregnant.

Breasts: Although both men and women have breasts, during puberty a girl's breasts get larger. When a woman is pregnant her breasts make milk which may be used to feed the newborn baby.

Breech Birth: When a baby is born hips or buttocks first.

Cervix: The opening to a woman's uterus.

Cesarean Birth: When the newborn baby is lifted out of the mother's uterus through an opening made in her abdomen by the doctor.

Child Molester: A sex offender who is interested in children.

Circumcision: When the foreskin on the penis is removed by a doctor.

Clitoris: A tiny bud located where a woman's inner lips meet above her vagina.

Condom: A balloon-like covering placed over the penis to keep sperm from entering the vagina.

Contraceptive Foam: A foam squirted into the vagina to prevent sperm from reaching a woman's eggs.

Contractions: Tightening of the muscles of the uterus during labor.

Diaphragm: A rubber disc which is placed over the cervix to prevent a man's sperm from reaching a woman's eggs.

Ejaculation: When semen and sperm squirt out of a man's penis.

Erection: When a man's penis or a woman's clitoris becomes stiff.

Fallopian Tubes: The tubes that connect a woman's ovaries to her uterus.

Fantasy: A daydream.

Fertilization: When a man's sperm meets with a woman's egg and a baby begins to grow.

Foreskin: The skin which hangs over the end of an uncircumcised penis.

IUD: Intrauterine device. A birth control device inserted by a doctor into a woman's uterus to prevent her from becoming pregnant.

Labor: The work a woman does when she gives birth, pushing the baby out of the uterus and down through the vagina.

Lubrication: When the vagina gets wet because of sexual excitement.

Masturbation: Rubbing or touching one's own body for sexual pleasure, most often the sexual organs.

Menopause: The time in a woman's life when her menstrual periods stop.

Menstruation: When a girl becomes a young woman and, usually once a month, the lining of the uterus is discharged and a bloody discharge drips through the vagina.

Navel: The place where your umbilical cord connected you to your mother's placenta before you were born.

Orgasm: A very strong feeling of pleasure during sexual activity.

Ova: The eggs inside a woman's body. One egg is an **Ovum.**

Ovaries: The two glands inside a woman's body which produce the ova.

Penis: A man's sex organ.

Placenta: The organ inside the mother's uterus to which the umbilical cord is connected.

Pregnancy: When a woman has a baby growing in her uterus.

Premature Birth: When a baby is born too early or is too small.

Prostate Gland: The gland inside a man's body where semen is made.

Puberty: That time in a person's life when a boy begins to change into a man and a girl begins to change into a woman.

Rubber: See *Condom*.

Sanitary Napkin: A pad worn by a woman during menstruation to keep the bloody discharge from staining her clothes.

Semen: A whitish, sticky fluid containing sperm.

Sex Offender: When a person forces you to engage in sexual activity with them when you do not wish to.

Sexual Intercourse: When a man's penis enters a woman's vagina.

Sperm: The millions of tiny organisms made in a man's testicles. When a sperm meets a woman's egg, a baby begins to grow.

Tampon: A small pad which is inserted into the vagina to keep the bloody discharge from staining a woman's clothes during menstruation.

Testicles: The glands in a man which produce sperm.

Umbilical Cord: The cord that connected you to your mother's placenta before you were born.

Urethra: The tube in men and women through which urine passes. In men it is the same tube through which semen is ejaculated.

Uterus: The organ inside a woman's body where a baby grows.

Vagina: A woman's sex organ.

VD (Venereal Disease): Any disease caught by having close sexual contact with people who have VD germs.

Wet Dream: Having an orgasm while you sleep.

Index

About the Authors

John W. Petras, Professor of Sociology at Central Michigan University, earned his Ph.D. at the University of Connecticut. He has written numerous articles and is the author or co-author of eight books, among them *Sexuality in Society* and *The Social Meaning of Human Sexuality*. A Certified Sex Educator, he has also conducted workshops on sex education and is co-developer and instructor of an interdisciplinary, introductory sexuality course at Central Michigan University. He is co-developer and instructor with Loren Burt, M.D., of the nation's first combination adult education college credit sexuality class.

Jennifer J. Aho is research associate with John W. Petras on the sexual awareness of children and has conducted, with Dr. Petras, sex education workshops aimed at parents, teachers, physicians and medical personnel. She is a teaching assistant in college-level human sexuality classes at Central Michigan University. Her main area of concentration is the sexual nature and sex role development of children.